About The Author

Ever since I was twelve years old, I have adored telling stories in some way shape or form. Whether it was through bands I was in or through my YouTube/Twitch live streaming days. I always wanted other people to live inside my head and experience the strange things I could conjure. I recall the first time I saw a horror movie. It was the TV mini series adaption of Stephen King's 'Salem's Lot' which was later released as a movie on VHS. I became obsessed with it, but at the same time it scared the living shit out of me. I dreamt about vampires (specifically Barlow) trying to hunt me down in the house where I lived. I even taped make-shift crosses to my window to warn off vampires.
I lived in the real Ilfracombe, laid out in this book, and it equally scared the shit out of me. There was an atmosphere quite unlike anywhere else, a strange sadness or emptiness about it. I also grew up in Ilfracombe around the same time as

many notable fires that had happened due to the old victorian system the town was built on.
I always believed the town would make a great setting for a horror story, and I have over the years attempted to write this story several times.
So now as i write this in 2025, i am 35 years old, *why did it take me so long?*
When i was in year 11 and due to start my GCSE's, I had to write a creative writing piece, it could be about anything I wanted, and it excited me to the point where I had written a novella titled "Rise of the Dead" It was a sequel to George A Romero's zombie movies. I remember finishing it and being so proud of what I had achieved, I enjoyed the process from start to finish. I decided it was what I was going to do for the rest of my life.
Life had a different plan, my english teacher at the time graded it an A* piece of work. But then decided that it had to be plagiarism, because it was better than the rest of my work and told me that he wouldn't accept it and that I would be in major trouble with the headteacher.
They could never prove that it was (because it wasn't) and my parents were getting divorced, and so the attention from me at that point was just to be purely rebellious, I didn't pick up another book to even read until years later and I had convinced myself I wasn't a good writer at all. If I could say one thing to that fourteen/fifteen year old me, it would be "Try and get the thing published and ignore the old asshole!"

For Rebecca, the light in my darkness.

"The house was a monument to evil, sitting there all these years holding the essence of evil in its smoldering bones." - Stephen King 'Salem's Lot'

1

PRESENT DAY

Anticipation twisted in the pit of Sam's stomach. An old, unwelcome sensation. Like an acquaintance she'd hoped never to meet again. Her knees trembled, hands tucked between them, her mouth dry despite the mint she'd nursed for half an hour.
She was tired of the road, of waiting for a safe haven, a warm bed. But mostly, she was tired of the heavy quiet that trailed her like a shadow.
They had left the orphanage around two o'clock on a drizzly Monday afternoon. Autumn had only just begun to show its creeping death—leaves browned, flowers withered, and the nights grew longer.
The driver had been mute for the entire journey, breaking the silence only with the occasional cough. There was no radio either, which somehow made the ride all the more excruciating. In the backseat, she felt every bump and dip of the country roads.
A numbness had crept in early during the journey, carried in with every shudder and vibration of the car. The seats were comfortable at first. However the faux leather did little to support her posture for long.

Sam barely noticed the car slowing down. Despite her nerves about the destination, she couldn't wait to stand and stretch.
A signpost flicked past the window: *Ilfracombe*.
Strange name.
This was the first time Sam would come to live in such a remote place, she tried to remember how the lady at the orphanage had pronounced the name.
Ill-fra-coom?
Cliffs, laced with the tops of trees, sat on the horizon. Dead trees and leaves littered every pavement, and long, unkempt grass spilled across the roadside.
They followed a narrow road, flanked by overgrown stone walls that loomed above the verge. Every few yards, signs warned of landslides and falling rocks. To the right, a steep drop opened into jagged rock and woodland below. Sam imagined the car veering off the edge and quickly looked away.
Sam leaned forward, pressing her palm to the seat. The leather warmed quickly under her sweaty hand. She was trying to get a better view ahead, constricted by the side view of the window beside her.
A cluster of houses came into view, white picket fences, long driveways, neatly trimmed hedges, all perched on a hill overlooking the endless horizon.
Sam's heart sank, they weren't stopping.
The car continued around a long bend, approaching a roundabout. On the right sat a recycling center, its steel gates chained shut, as if it had never opened at all.

Another bend in the road revealed the town below, nestled at the top of a hill. Beyond it, a dark blue ocean faded into a white, mist-heavy horizon.

As they passed through the town's high street, she noticed the buildings were old and weathered by time. Once a bustling English beach town in the summer, it sat eerily still.

Now they were closer to civilisation, (if you could call this place civilisation) the radio sprung to life, it took the driver by surprise and it made Sam jump out of her skin. It had seemingly found a station and it was now playing 'The Doors - People are Strange' a very fitting soundtrack as Sam would later discover.

Losing count of the bed and breakfast signs along this stretch of the road she moved her face closer to the window to see past her reflection. She was thinner than most girls her age. Her thin-rimmed glasses hung low on her nose, and she constantly pushed them back up.

She found her own reflection unpleasant, despite never being taunted about her looks. It would remind her of all the negative things about herself. She struggled to let go of the past, especially the bad parts, as they stuck out like a sore thumb. She pressed her nose against the glass.

In place of tourists, a few old people wandered the streets. They moved in short, shuffling bursts across dirty pavements stained with bird droppings and colourful litter.

Watching people in their daily lives. She did it often at school—well, when she was in attendance. The last school day blurred into Gabbie Tyrone's fist. A sharp yank of her hair. A punch to the gut. And still, Sam got the blame.

"Lazy" the teachers said. "Moody" "Difficult" But her silence had always screamed the loudest and no one ever listened.

This was her fifth home and her fifth "problematic" label from the care system.

Adults always said she was too clever, too outspoken, too opinionated. Children should be seen and not heard.

Sam was happy to leave her last foster home. Mr. Forester, her previous caregiver, was an old, seedy man whose hands often ventured into places they shouldn't. If she had pushed him away, Sam would be punished through deprivation: no food, no electricity, and no TV. On the final occasion (after slapping him for touching her) she was accused of being too aggressive.

Just weeks later he was caught trying to entice a young girl on the way home from school and was in the papers.

On the move again—not by choice.

Brushing away the dark memories using her usual technique, Sam pictured a large box and stuffed all the darkness into it. She locked it with chains, and pushed it out of sight. As she opened her eyes, the car's brakes squealed over a gravel surface.

Sam had arrived at her new home.

She swung herself out of the backseat and caught her green cardigan on the door latch with a loud rip. She barely noticed, it was just another hole in one of the two cardigans she owned.

The silent, nameless driver dropped her suitcase in front of her, got back into the car, and drove away without checking if she could get inside. Quickly leaving a plume of dust that blocked her vision for a moment.

She tried to compose herself before looking at the place she'd be staying. She always imagined the worst-case scenario, but to her surprise, the house was beautiful. It was a mansion—one of the largest she'd ever seen. There were too many windows to count, and the front had large wooden double doors, reminiscent of a church. Above the door was a faded coat of arms.

Sam couldn't make out the details,maybe a bird or a lizard? It was hard to tell; the years had worn it down.

She could smell the fresh sea air, the gulls crying out overhead as they landed with a thud on the rooftop high above.

Her gaze shifted to the far right of the house, where it stretched around a corner, disappearing through the trees. She noticed a modern section had been added. Then her eyes caught on a stained-glass window that stole all her attention.

There was a metallic clunking sound from the other side of the doors, they creaked outwards slowly. What seemed like forever was only a second or two.

Sam felt her heart jump into her throat, a trickle of cold sweat on her brow, and a buzzing in her lungs as a figure appeared from the doorway.

2

The anxiety in Sam's chest settled into a tight, quiet shyness. Or perhaps a forced politeness, shaped by years of navigating strangers. Sam locked her gaze on the ground and swallowed the lump in her throat.
From the corner of her eye, she saw a tall, thin woman step out from the doorway. She could smell the strong perfume even standing a few feet away. It was a scent of fresh linen wrapped up with a hint of orange and a touch of vanilla. It was pleasant to Sam and quite inviting.
"Hello"
A strong voice, not masculine or feminine. It was confident though and straight to the point.
Sam lifted her head and smiled instantly in response and greeted a hello back in return.
The woman was ghastly-looking— so thin that her features seemed almost jagged, as though her face had pointed accents that could cut through metal. Her eyes withered.
Sam felt an instant guilt for thinking this way.
She often lived with two voices in her head. One of them was judgemental, mostly born from her traumatic upbringing by persons on either side of the morality spectrum.
The other was certainly that of an ordinary girl that was on the cusp of Sixteen. The other voice often walked over.
The woman wore a black velvet dress with a white trim. A

necklace hung low that looked like something Sam might find in a tacky gift shop. It looked like a nest of twigs holding a green gem, perhaps it could be expensive, Sam wasn't exactly knowledgeable but it did seem on the tackier, cheaper side. Maybe even home-made. It reflected sunlight and cast a small light against the brickwork.
The woman turned her back, walked a few paces back into the doorway, and then turned with a slight pause.
"Well are you just going to stand there?"
The woman was emotionless, it couldn't be read as either mockery, amusement or anger.
"No, Sorry…Umm"
Sam was growing more nervous at the lady's tone and unpredictability, she had known her for a mere minute and she had a gut feeling it wasn't going to be a pleasant place to stay. She tried to stay positive, perhaps she would find this place to be a comfort.
Sam followed her guidance through the doorway, her suitcase uncontrolled over the stones and onto the small section of stone flooring in the entryway.
The warm air inside wrapped around her like a blanket, scented with smoke, jasmine, and something faintly floral. The fireplace crackled, casting a soft glow in the otherwise pale daylight.
The room she was now standing in, was immediately beyond the front doors and seemed to be a reception room of sorts; it could have easily been a hotel lobby at some point in its seemingly long history.

Sam wanted to correct the lop-sided paintings and photographs on the wall, which reflected the history.
There was a small sofa, it seemed to be aged and quite tatty looking, a grey knitted throw was covering the seats but it didn't hide the frayed threads. Sam had never seen a sofa with tassels around the bottom and touching the dull grey carpet it rested on.
 "My name is Miss Parr, and I expect to be addressed this way, you understand?"
"Yes Miss Parr"
Miss Parr stood straight, there was no curve in her spine or so it seemed that way. One arm behind her back, like she was concealing something, but it was just her posture when projecting authority.
"Samantha, I'll show you to your room"
Sam internally cringed at the use of her long name, nobody had ever called her that before. She had only seen it on official documents at the Orphanage. She didn't correct her though.. Perhaps in time.
The ceilings were low, and from inside, it didn't seem quite as beautiful. Most of the curtains were half-closed, letting small beams of light pierce the room and illuminate thick dust dancing through it, as though trying to escape.
Glancing over at a small clock hanging high up on the wall above the sofa. Five o'clock.. The journey was not as long as she he originally thought but she was tired nevertheless.
Taking a left and still following behind Miss Parr, they passed several doors, there were no numbers or any indication of

what was beyond them. Sam immediately felt quite excited at this mystery.

They proceeded down another hallway. It was hard to tell where they were now—the corridors in the house were all identical and unspectacular, with a long burgundy (or possibly red, but caked in dust) carpet down the middle with gold borders, exposed floorboards on either side, and the occasional wall lamp between doors.

As they walked past an open door, Sam caught a glimpse—and it was horrible. She wished she hadn't looked. All she saw was a glass cabinet full of old Victorian dolls. And it was like they were watching her pass by.

"Do you live here alone, Miss Parr?" Sam felt a little more confident asking a question as they continued down a corridor that didn't seem to end.

Miss Parr turned her head, not directly at Sam and turned up her nose again. "Yes. Well, there used to be the groundskeeper, but he left some time ago. It's just me and whichever child they send me next."

With her mind racing, Sam couldn't believe she was alone with Miss Parr in this huge house. It was daunting. Why did she need all this space to herself?

"This is a big house, Miss Parr. How many rooms are there?" Sam continued, her confidence growing after the non-threatening reply last time.

"There are fifty two rooms over three floors. And then there is the newly built east wing, That is where I spend most of my time."

Sam said nothing, taking in the information, trying to slowly get her bearings.

"You will stay on the top floor in the oldest part of the house. That way I can have my peace and quiet."

At that moment, Miss Parr suddenly stopped in her tracks. She fixed her eyes on a dark room.

"Are you OK, Miss?" Sam leaned into the room a little to see if she could see what it was Miss Parr was staring at, but she had snapped back out of it quite quickly.

"This way"

They turned the corner of the corridor and passed by a large room.

It was a dining room, and it looked almost regal. It had large paintings of noble-looking figures. There was a suit of armour in the corner of the room, and Sam felt like she was suddenly in a historic castle-turned-museum, one that she would often visit with her second placement carers.

It was becoming impossible to obtain any sense of bearings or direction. Sam was following Miss Parr, through endless corridors and up several flights of stairs. Wishing there was a lift they could use and save her small amount of energy she had remaining.

Finally after three or four flights, several identical corridors and through a heavy modern firedoor that seemed out of place. They arrived at a rickety wooden staircase that led up to a light oak coloured door that was different to the rest of the house. As they climbed the steps, she felt unsteady as the stairs seemed to rock slightly. It didn't seem to phase Miss

Parr and so Sam felt reassured she wasn't about to come crashing down amongst splinters of broken wooden planks. Opening the door revealed a small room that was clearly once the loft space. Sam immediately thought of the words *attic room* remembering that she read about a similar room in an American novel once.

The floorboards were dusty and much more worn out than most of the house she'd seen, the walls were sloped and old wooden beams sat parallel.

Against the wall, facing a small single bed was an old, large wardrobe with holes where the handles should be. It was a creepy-looking thing with hand-carved cherubs in the corners of the doors. Their faces looked anguished and pained, twisted mouths like they were reaching from the depths of hell for help. Sam didn't like it at all.

On the bedside table sat a bright yellow alarm clock with a clown face. It was cheerful and absurd against the room's gloom, like a joke left behind by someone with a cruel sense of humour.

This was far from a comfortable space for Sam, but it was somewhere to rest, somewhere she could think for herself. It was somewhere for her to daydream about her future, her hopes and her dreams.

3

Almost five thirty, the sun was still attempting to cut through the clouds, in through the single pane slanted roof window, and was now lighting a small section of Sam's new bedroom. She was still holding onto the handle of her small blue suitcase, she only had a few items. A couple of t-shirts, jeans, pajamas, socks and underwear.. She had a small elephant plushie that she had held onto since her first memories.
"Unpack your things, then you'll clean yourself up before dinner"
Before Sam could respond, Miss Parr was out of the door and stampeding down the steps, her footsteps heavy for her thin frame.
At the end of the bed sat an oak ottoman, strangely the only thing in the room untouched by dust. She lifted the lid to find it completely empty and so proceeded to unzip her case and place her clothes inside.
She stopped as she picked up her elephant. She had named it Ronnie in recent years. Named after a cat she befriended at the orphanage. She missed Ronnie a huge deal, she'd often take scraps of her food to him and tell him about her day. She thought it was stupid at first, a cat being the only thing to confide in. Eventually it seemed normal to her, she would continue to talk to him in more detail with each passing week. A sense of loneliness had crossed her mind, she glanced

around the room and felt that it had no touch of her own personality. She longed for a time where she would have a bedroom, and decorate it with her own things. Never having that was upsetting-let alone having no money to buy things for herself.
She dreaded Christmas, the autumnal feeling that day reminded her of its impending smothering nature. She would often watch children from afar across the street from the Orphanage. They would be alongside their natural birth parents. Excitingly looking in shop windows and eyeing what they wanted that year. She never really had the chance to experience a magical Christmas with a family of her own.
maybe - one day.
Five minutes to six, the clown faced clock smiling at her, it made her feel uneasy. It reminded her of something that she couldn't quite place at that moment. Perhaps close to the feeling of deja vu.
Footsteps faded in front the floors below, at first a slight pitter patter that quickly grew into a stomping.
Miss Parr entered the room with a dominant-like force. She quickly glanced around the room, expecting something to be out of place and then looked at Sam.
"Time for a bath"
Again snappy, to the point and wasted no time to leave the room. Sam hurried to her feet and grabbed some clothes from the ottoman before she was interrupted. Miss Parr's face peered from around the corner of the doorway.
"Leave those, you'll not need those grubby things"

Sam felt insulted, but again not confident and maybe not silly enough to respond in any defence, and she thought to herself that her clothes were ill-fitting these days, she was quickly growing out of them and perhaps she had something nicer.

Led down the rickety stairs and down a long corridor again. She lost count of the doors she passed, but remained on the fourth floor. Guided into another bedroom with an ensuite, she was faced with a steel bathtub with two pale taps.

"Perhaps we'll throw away those clothes of yours. I will fetch you something more appropriate"

The door slammed, and Sam was alone.

She turned the hot tap, it didn't flow smoothly and more like a leaking pipe. As she slowly took off her clothes, she noticed the scars on her shoulders. For a brief second, she was back there, flashing before her eyes. She saw the belt flying toward her in slow motion. It was her father's belt, and she remembered the pain with every lashing. She could smell the leather and hear the air being slashed by its force.

Then she saw it—the ashtray. It was memorable because it was thick marble and uniquely hand-crafted.

Quickly pulling herself out of that moment, she thought to herself:

Something I can touch: the steel bathtub.

Something I can see: the still water and the bubbles floating upon it.

Something I can taste: the mint I had on the way here still lingers.

Something I can smell: the musty air—there wasn't much

else to smell.
Something I can hear... wait, nothing. I can hear nothing.

It was a technique she learnt from a therapist assigned to her at the orphanage. She rather enjoyed her company, she was able to spill things that she wouldn't often speak of to the other children or social workers.
Panic began to roll over her like a thunderous cloud overhead. Darkness crept into her peripheral vision, and a ringing slowly rose in her ears, growing louder and louder. Climbing into the tub and focused on the sound of the splashing water as she sat down, knees hugged to her chest. She felt safer this way. As she took several deep breaths, the ringing began to subside, and her vision cleared.
Sam had really learned how to regulate her emotions, but when she couldn't quickly find a distraction, panic always took hold. She began to feel numb, like she didn't exist, like she was floating outside her body. She would have to pinch the skin on her forearm to feel something, and if she didn't, she would feel like she was losing control.
Sam lowered herself into the water, allowing the bath to fill around her. It was piping hot, but that's how she liked it.
As her eyes adjusted to the darkness, Sam began to notice the room around her. Floral wallpaper from what she assumed to be pre-second world war or older, torn in places, occasionally revealed crumbling walls with exposed wood panels. There was a painting of a tree, backlit by a purple night sky. A campfire burned in front of the tree, casting light on the

twisted trunk. The tree looked unnatural, its branches reaching out like tortured souls.
The room's remainder was equally weathered and worn.
There was a side table with a small closed drawer, and Sam's imagination ran wild with what could be inside.
Now starting to relax, her knees dropped lower, her legs sinking into the water. Admitting to herself that it was nice to have a bath. Sam often enjoyed bathing. But thanks to her so-called previous caregiver, she'd never felt safe enough to bathe in his home.

She loved the only placement she was given.
Mr. and Mrs. Thompson from Exeter were a lovely husband and wife who couldn't have children. They welcomed Sam with open arms.
It ended abruptly in a horrible accident. Mrs. Thompson lost control of her car and ploughed into an icy lake. Mr. Thompson stopped eating, talking, or doing anything at all for a long while. He was unable to keep up with bills and they had to move into a smaller flat. One day, the social workers came knocking. They took Sam away against her will and his. Lengthy battles ensued to bring her back to him, but all talks broke down abruptly and she never understood why. Later he decided he wanted to be with his wife and hung himself—writing Sam a letter confessing his anger at the system for failing her.
After another six months of living in an orphanage while they tried to find another placement, she eventually landed with

Mr. Hodgkins. He was a history teacher with a severe drinking problem. He never harmed Sam physically, but he would shout, scream, and hurl foul words every night after returning from the pub.
Sinking deeper into the water, thinking about Mr. and Mrs. Thompson, she remembered how kind they had been—how Mrs. Thompson would plait her hair while singing, "Hush, little baby…"
Sinking further into the water to wash her long, matted brown hair. It definitely needed cutting, but she never had the opportunity, and she certainly didn't have the money to go to a professional. Most of the time, she would cut it herself when it became an annoyance.

Now submerged, the lullaby played in her mind:

Hush, little baby, don't say a word, Mama's gonna buy you a mockingbird…

Miss Parr's piercing gaze interrupted her precious memories as she opened her eyes, seeing them rippled in the water.. Her face was twisted and distorted, terrifying Sam to the point where she couldn't move for a second.
"Hurry up, girl. Here are some clothes. They fit the last one. I think these will do," Miss Parr said as Sam resurfaced with a panicked breath.
"What's wrong with you?"
"You just startled me, Miss. I didn't hear you come in,"

Wiping the water from her eyes. She grabbed the towel from the floor by the tub and wrapped it around herself.

"Silly girl. dress, and you'll have dinner before your evening chores"

Miss Parr said, beginning to leave the room, she stopped and remembered her curious face from earlier.

"Don't go wandering. It would be very rude. There are only a few places you are allowed to go. There's no need for anywhere else unless I say. Is that understood, girl?"

Closing the door slightly but not all the way. She moved back into the room, eyes fixed on Sam like a vulture on its prey. Half nodding, still startled by Miss Parr's sudden appearance. Wrapping a towel around herself, she yanked on the plug in the bath and watched the whirlpool pull away the still steaming water into the drain.

Sam turned and picked up the dress given to her, a navy-blue dress with white trim. Similar to Miss Parr's. It smelled old and musty, just like the house. As she examined it, she noticed a small, scrunched-up slip of paper in the pocket. She unraveled it behind her back, careful not to be seen.

The word *Violet*—scribbled in black ink.

4

Sam guessed at the time, it must have been around six fifteen to six thirty. She was now being guided back to the dining room they passed before, which was several floors below the bath she just thoroughly enjoyed.
They passed a window which exposed the dark blue sky, the night was drawing in now.
As they approached the familiar regal dining room, which housed the spooky suit of armour she remembered seeing in scooby doo cartoons, she felt uneasy for just a moment. It wasn't Miss Parr, it felt like something had walked past her, she felt the air circulate around her. There was nobody else around.
The train of thought was immediately broken, distracted by the decorations in the dining room. A large dark well varnished and Sam assumed an *antique* table sat in the middle of the room.
"Sit, I'll fetch something to eat"
Miss Parr quickly disappeared again, Sam's imagination at play wondering what kind of food she would be given. Not that she was fussed, she had eaten all kinds of foods. She had lived with a vegan foster carer as well as an older Japanese lady who would cook her things she didn't even know the

name of.

All she knew at that moment was that she was very hungry. She hadn't eaten since the morning at the orphanage.

She sat in on a large and rather heavy chair, she had to use a lot of her strength to pull the chair out to sit down, it made a horrific low scraping noise as the feet scraped along the wooden floor. The chair reminded her of a throne that a great king might sit upon, there was another at the far end of the table that was identical, it had intricate hand carved swirls and shapes, finished off with a dark varnish.

A smell rushed up the staircase now, something was cooking and there was a vegetable smell, it first smelt quite delicious but a worrying stench of foul cabbage quickly accompanied it. Sam sat at the table patiently, still observing the room around her. The suit of armour was just behind her right shoulder. She felt like it was watching her, making sure she wouldn't misbehave in the old lady's absence.

There was a huge painting sitting between two windows, a long dark haired man, clean shaven, with a quill in his left hand, and a book under his right arm. emotionless expression, eyes locking onto Sam's and she felt uncomfortable the further she stared back. She disliked those old paintings where the eyes would follow you around the room. There were many of these that littered the walls of the house and she dreaded the thought of seeing them in the dark. Luckily none of these hung in her bedroom. But then remembering the terrifying cherub wardrobe, *that will be very creepy in the dark.*

Occasionally, an open door out of sight would create a

bubbling and hissing noise. Clearly the sounds of the old lady cooking up the food as the smell would drift again in unison with the sound of the door.
The dining room was silent, a small metallic tinkling sound came from her right shoulder, looking over to react, It was coming from the armour. Her eyes fixed on it, waiting for it to move or make another sound. It never came to pass.
She brushed it off to being an old house of course, so many things caked in dust are bound to create small noises around the unsettled wood.
She felt uneasy again now, peering over her other shoulder into the doorway. She felt as though something was standing there watching her. She couldn't see anything but she felt a presence.
Never believing in ghosts and never experiencing this feeling before, it was alien to her at this moment. She had rather enjoyed the ghost stories her friends would tell each other in the dark. They would often sneak out of their bunks, gather in the middle of the room and tell stories under the moonlight. It was certainly the right setting to be haunted, but she laughed to herself quietly at the silliness of such things and turned back around facing the other empty chair.

The clock chimed repeatedly from downstairs, she counted them. Seven o'clock. The room was dark now as the sun had completely vanished.
The chandelier erupted with light with a clicking of the switch behind her. Miss Parr walked into the room with a bowl and

cutlery, she said nothing, placing it down in front of her, making sure it was neat and the cutlery was placed appropriately. She did the same on her side of the table and then vanished from the room again.

It wasn't long before she re-appeared with a large pan, she scooped out a ladle of hot stew and poured it into the bowl in front of Sam, she did the same for herself and then walked out of the room with the large steel pan.

The stew was brown, with green leaves floating on its surface. There were chunks of meat but she was unsure what animal it was from. There was an occasional slice of carrot that bobbed to the surface.

It didn't look terrible, but it was far from Mrs Thompson's famous Lasagne that was often celebrated on a Thursday night, after her spin class.

Miss Parr came back with a basket of bread, placed it in front of Sam, who was now excited as they were warm table rolls, she loved those.

Walking over and effortlessly pushing back the chair to sit down, she placed a napkin over her thighs and looked dead pan at Sam, waiting for her to do the same.

A split second and Sam realized she had to do this, smiled and continued to do so.

Eat the stew there. It's delicious, I promise you."

This was the first time she smiled, but it wasn't a nice smile—it was a smirk from the corner of her mouth.

She expected some conversation, but it was just awkward silence to Sam throughout the entire meal. Silence was broken

by the slurping from the other side of the table.
She still couldn't determine the meat, it wasn't chicken, it could be lamb, or *maybe turkey?* It was flavourless and chewy. But the bread was delicious, she made sure to eat all of it.
"I will take you to the library when you are finished, where you will re-alphabetise my books. You understand?"
This time Miss Parr wasn't looking at her; she was looking out of the window, unsure what it was she was staring at, it was now pitch black and no moonlight, it was easier to just study the reflection of the room in the glass pane, Sam avoided this as usual though.
She has a library
 Sam couldn't believe it. What else was hiding in this house that she didn't know about? Her wildest thoughts were going through her mind. Maybe she had a swimming pool? A games room?
Before she knew it, Sam had finished her stew. Along with all the bread, leaving no crumbs. It was the most full she had felt in some time, and she was starting to feel tired from it.
With the sound of a low drag, Miss Parr rose to her feet, her ankles clicking with age or possibly arthritis. She took away her bowl and cutlery and clicked her fingers at Sam.
"Follow, bring yours"
Snappy again, Sam didn't like the tone at all, but did as instructed and stood up quickly, using all her energy to push the chair back with her legs.
Sam followed Miss Parr downstairs to the Kitchen, it wasn't far and the Kitchen itself was tiny for how big the house was,

just a small box room.

The walls were split, the top half were an off white, slightly textured paint. The bottom half was tiled royal blue, some of the tiles were chipped and cracked.

On one side of the kitchen was just empty counter space, white cupboards underneath and above on the wall. These were also slightly off white and slightly dirty looking, but mostly scuffed with years of usage.

The other side of the kitchen had a small thin window, next to this a large cabinet of China. The kind of china you would expect an old lady to collect, it was blue and white with some kind of illustration and patterns around the edges. They all matched.

She pointed at the end of the room, at a white ceramic double sink with a draining board, it was immaculately clean, a large crack spread across the back of the sink near the steel grey taps.

"Wash those please, quickly"

Sam wasted no time on the instruction, she walked over the blue tiled floor which felt slightly sticky under feet. Miss Parr seemed to take a mental note as she watched her feet.

Turning the tap, it was grinding against the metal, she felt grit in each turn and water gushed out of the pipe, she tested the water which was cold and waited a moment until it warmed. Proceeding to wash the bowls and cutlery carefully, making sure she didn't miss anything. She placed the sopping, dripping wares onto the draining board and looked at Miss Parr for another instruction.

A small black figure creeped around the doorway, Sam was delighted to see a cat and thought immediately about Ronnie. The cat stopped and glared at her, its piercing green eyes actually unnerved her a little, the cat walked towards his food bowl and sat patiently waiting.
"This is Artemis"
Miss Parr expressed her only genuine smile, she squatted and stroked Artemis' black coat, he began to purr and move his head around her palm, eyes squinted in delight.
Miss Parr took out a pouch of Royal Canin cat food from one of the cupboards below the counter, she peeled off the top and poured it into Artemis blue bowl that was matching the tiled walls and floor.
"I am only to feed him"

5

"To the library. Follow me."

She shouted as she spun on her heel, marching ahead out of the door almost like a soldier in military fashion, and Sam followed.

Walking down and back into the lobby. past a set of much cleaner double doors. Miss Parr stood in front of them, using her arms to shield any sight of what was beyond them.

"That is where I spend my time. You are not permitted there. You are not permitted to even look beyond these doors."

She looked stern and more serious than anyone Sam had ever seen. Miss Parr had again remembered Sam's curious look from earlier in the day.

They turned a corner, and then, as they reached the end of another blandly decorated corridor, Miss Parr burst excitedly through another set of doors, like she was about to surprise someone.

"Here we are, my pride and joy. My library. These are my very own children,"

She almost waltzed around the room, spinning on her heel again and, in a trance, flailing her arms around.

"As you can see, the books go out of order very easily because I read them all the time and, well, one does not have the time to reorganise."

She had now stopped her crazy waltz and was standing,

staring at Sam, towering over her like a dragon ready to snarl fire and steam.

To Sam, Miss Parr reminded her of Miss Trunchbull from the film Matilda—only if she had lost a significant amount of weight. And yes, it's not the book, she didn't read the book. She never read books because she never had the time to herself to do so. But they often played films like Matilda and Charlie & The Chocolate Factory at the orphanage.

"Well, come on,"

Miss Parr said as she snapped her fingers in all directions. "These books will not organize themselves. Now you can start however you like. I just want them organised within the next couple of hours. When I come back, I expect it to be done so I can take you to your room for bed."

Before Sam could even acknowledge her, she had gone and slammed the doors behind her. You couldn't even hear her walking away down the corridor, it had gone eerily silent once again.

Sam brushed the many piles of stacked books, some of which were caked in dust, as she paced around the room. Someone knocked over some of the piles, like a lost game of Jenga.

She then heard a small, faint tapping sound from behind her. Moving closer towards the sound and past an ornamental globe—the kind you'd see in rich people's houses in the films, like old gangster films where the mob boss had his own office.

There was a piano too. The lid was lifted, exposing the bright white keys that were surprisingly polished and clean, free from dust.

Something tore the silence in the room apart. Sam's heart fluttered as a dark grey mass slammed down onto the piano, glaring eyes piercing her and fangs of a horrific beast-like nature.

It was another cat. a horrifically ugly, pure grey cat. Ugly because it had scars across its face, and one eye permanently closed shut which seemed to be oozing something from the corner of its eye. It had jumped onto the piano, playing the low notes with its paws on impact. It was hissing at Sam with its back arched. It had some teeth missing as well. Sam, at this point, was walking backwards, and after a low rumbling growl, the cat had run past her and out of sight.

Gently picking up the books and being careful not to damage anything, she wondered how many cats lived there.

Sam began to place the books on the shelves in alphabetical order. After briefly reading some of the titles—which sounded very dull. *The Complete Encyclopedia of Medieval Plantlife in Britain* and *The Healing Powers of Lemon Balm.* She picked up the pace to make sure she had completed her chores in time for Miss Parr's return.

She stopped as she read a few paragraphs of a *Bram Stoker's Dracula.* Deciding already it was way too creepy for her, let alone during the night in a big spooky house.

Then that thought re-occurred to her, validating herself, it was in fact a spooky house. It was causing an uneasy nervous feeling in her stomach, similar to the feeling of anticipation she felt on arrival.

Sam continued to take books from random piles. Sorting them

into alphabetical order, which seemed to be more difficult considering some of the books were so aged. She had to open them and discover the titles.

In doing so, one of the books strangely rattled upon picking it up. The book looked ordinary enough at first glance. A faded cloth-bound tome with frayed corners and the faint, musty scent of old paper. But when she opened it, the pages resisted, stiff and unnatural. Inside, the heart of the book had been hollowed out with surgical precision. A secret cavity, neatly carved between the lines of forgotten text, cradled a single iron key. It lay nestled in the void like a relic in a tomb, waiting.

She looked around the room, looking for what this key could unlock, she wasn't sure. It excited her, it was like a real mystery she could attempt to solve. Miss Parr clearly didn't want it to be found with ease, but she obviously had made a mistake in leaving it for her to find. Or.. *perhaps she was meant to find it?*

She placed the book in a spot on the shelf where she would remember its location. Sam continued to organize the books, she thought she was making good headway. Until she noticed more piles of books in the corner, behind the door.

She noticed the ugly grey cat was sitting watching her from the end of the corridor outside, she took a moment to lock eyes with it, eventually it stood and walked out of sight again. *Yeah, you keep walking.*

Sam had finished the piles in front of her now, she had individual piles of books for each letter of the alphabet.. She headed over to the stack of hardbacks behind the door and began to sort through them.

The clock chimed eight, Sam was now placing the piles of books she had made into the right order on the shelves. She had to use a wooden ladder to reach the top, she hated it. She didn't like heights, and even climbing a small ladder was quite a terrifying chore.
She thought about the doorway she was instructed not to go through.
What was she hiding?
Sam coughed, she felt clean before messing with the books and now she had felt dusty, her horrifically uncomfortable dress had collected dust too.
She hated wearing dresses, Sam was one for jeans and t-shirt, with a cardigan in the autumn and winter.
The doors flung open and Miss Parr was carrying the ugly cat in her arms. It was purring away loudly, it took a gaze at Sam and dived out of her grasp, running back into the corridor.
"Remus doesn't like you, it seems"
She didn't look impressed, watching the cat scarper out of sight down the corridor.
She glanced at the neatly arranged books on the shelf, she didn't show any signs of affection or gratitude.
She walked towards the bookcase, and picked out a grey book, placing it under her arm. Sam recognised it as the book with the key and the old lady was staring at her suspiciously.
"Right, off to bed with you, I trust you remember your way"

Sam gulped, she couldn't remember, but it couldn't be too difficult, her room was at the very top of the house. She was glad to be getting some time to herself.
"I must not be disturbed"
Miss Parr walked away from the library, taking the same path as Remus earlier.

6

Sam began walking back to her room, starting with the doorless corridor that led out from the library. It felt claustrophobic, pressing in on both sides, but the feeling passed quickly as she stepped into the lobby.

Turning into the next corridor, she was met with a row of closed doors. three on each side and a staircase at the far end, veering off to the left. It was quiet. One of the wall lamps buzzed faintly, the sound of electricity whispering through the bones of the house.

She climbed the staircase. It was solid oak—not rickety like the one near her room. Broad and wide, it could easily accommodate two people passing in opposite directions without pause. A faded, patterned carpet ran up the steps like an old tongue rolling out toward something unseen.

At the top, the kitchen lay to her left. Familiar now, a flicker of reassurance. She passed windows overlooking the gravel car park and the treeline beyond. In the distance, across the road, she could just make out the holiday park. The small, run-down chalets were dark—off-season—but the streetlamps lit them in a strange, amber hush.

What caught her attention was a framed photograph beside the window. It showed the same view—but the building looked different. A crowd had gathered outside it, many pointing excitedly at a sign that read: North Devon Zoological Park &

Gardens.

She turned the next corner and froze. The door ahead was the one. The one with the dolls.

Even before reaching it, the presence of their gaze was felt. The cold prickle of unseen eyes.

Watching.

Waiting.

Swallowing a lump in her throat, forcing herself forward. She didn't look through the door. Her steps quickened as she passed, a rising urgency in her chest. She didn't want to be seen.

Not by them.

But the horror didn't end there.

Sam slowed to a stop—realizing, with a sinking feeling, that she'd taken a wrong turn.

She had to go back. Past that door.

Her stomach tightened. She turned, retracing her steps, forcing herself toward the hallway again. As she passed the dolls' room, a soft creak came from behind her—small, but deliberate.

Don't look.

Her breath caught, and then she broke into a run, rounding the corner in a blind rush, as though something might reach out and grab her the moment she hesitated.

She finally found the correct corridor, the one with windows overlooking a courtyard. In the middle of the overgrown square stood a stone fountain, cracked and weathered, with a goblin-like creature perched on top, frozen mid-leer. Around

the edge, weeds tangled through the beds of neglected plants, though some flowers still bloomed defiantly in the chaos.
At the far end of the corridor stood a black door. It was unlike any other door she'd seen in the house, older, maybe, or simply... wrong. Sam slowed. A chill crept up her spine. Something about it set her on edge.
Artemis was already there, sitting perfectly still in front of the door. His glowing eyes locked on hers, unblinking. Without moving his gaze, he lowered his head slowly to his paws, like a lion crouching to spring. His tail fluffed to twice its size, and a low, guttural growl rumbled from deep in his belly.
"Shoo! Get out of here, you horrible flea bag!" Sam snapped, her voice louder than she intended. She hadn't moved any closer.
Artemis didn't budge. He hissed, arching his back, eyes narrowed to slits. It wasn't a warning. It was a threat.
Ignoring it, Sam stepped forward. As she neared him, Artemis sprang aside with a screech, swiping at the air as she passed. His claws missed, but the message was clear.
Sam reached out and touched the door. It was freezing. An icy breeze leaked from the gap beneath it. She noticed a keyhole and crouched to peek through.
Darkness. Unlit candles. Shelves lined with books. A table in the middle of the room, draped with a sheet, something hidden beneath it.
Then, without warning, movement.
Something, or someone—passed just beyond the keyhole.
Sam gasped and fell backward, heart hammering.

Before she could recover, Artemis came hurtling through the air.

She screamed as his claws slashed her exposed ankle. The sting was instant, followed by a line of blood rising to the surface, vivid against her pale skin. Artemis vanished just as quickly, disappearing around the corner.

Sam clutched at her leg, grimacing. The cut wasn't deep, but it throbbed. Her mind returned to the room, the figure she'd seen. Maybe it was Miss Parr. Maybe she'd used the key Sam had found earlier.

"Miss Parr?" she called.

Silence.

Sam lingered only a moment, then shook it off and continued toward the staircase.

Through the fire door on the second floor. Past the dining room. A sharp glance at the looming suit of armour. She winced, half-expecting it to move.

Hooking around another corridor, she passed the bathroom where she'd bathed earlier and longed to be back in the safety of warm water.

Another fire door. *Had there been two before?* The layout blurred in her memory. This house twisted itself around her thoughts. A maze she couldn't quite map.

Finally, she reached the next staircase, narrower this time, leading up to the third floor. She remembered this. Just four rooms. One of them, a small box room, contained the final set of stairs to the attic level.

A painting hung here, a woman with her back to the viewer,

playing a violin. The sadness of it weighed on Sam. Maybe it was the colours: muted greys and blues bleeding into each other. Normally, a stained-glass window above would flood this space with colour. But now, with no lights on and no moonlight outside, the area lay in darkness.

She passed a doorway into a large open space beneath a hexagonal skylight. The glass above showed only blackness—no stars, no moon. Just a ceiling of void.

Then she found it: the rickety staircase, creaking softly under her steps as she climbed. At the top was her bedroom door. Safe. At last.

Pulling off her dress and swapping it for her long t-shirt that she would sleep in, she climbed into the bed, disappointed by how springy it was, she could feel the rusted springs as they bounced and squeeked with every move.

She closed her eyes, and thought of nothing but what might be ahead of her here under the eye of Miss Parr.

7

Rain began to pound against the window. From the top floor, Sam could hear it hammering the roof above the attic room. The floorboards were dusty, more worn than any she'd seen in the house.

     The bed, small and creaky, groaned with age; the springs once again grinding with a slight move or turn, and that worried Sam, as she would often fidget throughout the night. She was glad that it was raining, as she hated to sleep in absolute silence, and dreaded the first night doing so.

     A few moments passed without worry. She began to drift off. Something stirred at the edge of her mind, a thought... no, a feeling. That creeping sense of being watched again.

Her mind turned to the cherub faces that were probably staring at her from across the room, etched into the doors of the wardrobe.

She turned. She was right. They were there, staring at her through the darkness.

She sat for a while, staring straight back, until she decided to get up from bed and quickly tiptoe over with her horrid dress. She tried covering it, but the dress kept sliding off. Eventually, she gave up and walked back to her bed.

Tap… tap… tap…

Her eyes slowly opened once again, her breathing now unsteady and beginning to feel like she had just been sprinting from danger. Sam turned her head towards the window to the left of her — it was just a small single-paned window, quite dirty, briefly catching the glimpse of a crow's wing. Reassured, she turned away and closed her eyes again.
A few moments passed, and then again:

Tap... tap... tap...

Slowly sitting up, holding her bedsheets to her chest tightly in fear of what this strange sound was. Her body completely frozen, the hairs on her neck now stood to attention. The noises were loud enough to be heard over the rain.

It sounded like nails on glass.

Maybe it was Miss Parr coming to get her in the night, like a vampire at her window.

A few moments had passed, and she thought the sound had stopped and would not recur. But then again—this time, twice.

Tap... tap... tap...

then followed by a small but distinctive knock, and then again:

Tap… tap… tap…

Maybe it's the cat trying to get in.
The window did not open; there was no handle, and it was at roof level. She felt stupid for thinking it would be a cat, but then felt even more stupid for thinking it was a Vampire. There was nothing around the window that could be making that noise.

Sam got back into bed and pulled the covers over her so that she couldn't see what she felt could be preparing to get her—and so that whatever was making that noise couldn't see her.

You are being silly Sam.
Tap… tap… tap…
Why won't it stop?!

Folding the sides of the pillows over her ears now, she was terrified of every small noise. All rational sense had gone, she no longer thought about the settling wood in the autumnal weather, or the unstable rickety staircase that was probably moving in the breeze of what seemed to be a small storm brewing outside.

Sam eventually fell asleep.

Outside, beyond the glass, something shifted. But Sam, at last, did not see.

8

Sam jolted upright, arms flailing, heart racing, the sun beaming into her eyes. Unsure at first what had awoken her, she could hear heavy footsteps coming towards the door.

She should have been awake and dressed fifteen minutes ago, glancing at the smiling clock that stared back at her.

She jumped out of bed, and the old springs of the mattress sent her bouncing further. She flung her long t-shirt across the room and threw on her clothes. First her jogging bottoms, and then a light grey plain t-shirt. As the door slammed open and Miss Parr stood there, one hand behind her back and a familiar scowl on her face.

"Late again, I see. And what are you wearing? Your bed's a mess," she snapped, with one hand behind her back. Artemis was now sitting by her feet, staring at Sam like it knew she was in trouble and found it fun to watch.

"Don't look at Artemis. It's not his fault is it?" snapped Miss Parr, turning up her nose and moving her head aside and hissing her S's.

She was pacing around the room now, inspecting the

tidiness of the room, like a military inspection by a drill sergeant.

Looking at the floor anxiously, Sam couldn't help but wonder why Miss Parr wanted to take on foster children. Of course, there's the money aspect, but she seemed to dislike her.

She then realised Miss Parr had asked her a question and was staring at her, waiting.

"Well?"

"I'm sorry, Miss Parr, I didn't catch that,"
Her nervous feelings were taking control of her pitch again.
"Oh, so you are deaf as well, are you?" Miss Parr sniggered as she crossed her arms. "I said, I hope you're not afraid of spiders?" she continued to smirk.

"I am, Miss Parr," Sam said, being brutally honest — she absolutely hated them.

When she was much younger, she was playing hide and seek in the garden with some other foster children.

She decided to hide in a shed, and she was there for some time, squeezed in amongst a lawn mower, tools, rakes, and an assortment of garden things when the biggest spider she had ever seen crawled across her ankle.

She didn't dare move. It just sat there on her leg, staring — all its eyes locked on hers.

Sam snapped out of her memories, feeling like something was crawling on her. She nervously scratched the back of her neck and then checked her hand to make sure there wasn't an eight-legged monster there.

She followed Miss Parr nervously down to the lobby, there was a small door in the corner of the room that she hadn't noticed before. It seemed they were going below the ground floor.

"Here we are then," Miss Parr sneered and pointed into the darkness. It was a wine cellar, but Sam couldn't see how big the room was. It was pitch black, the kind of darkness where closing your eyes made no difference.

"Now, I want you to go and grab the mop and bucket from the back of this cellar and bring it up to the kitchen. While you mop the floor, I'll prepare breakfast." She spun and stormed up the stairs.

Knowing that Miss Parr had deliberately mentioned spiders to scare her, Sam felt even more afraid as she slowly walked into the darkness.

If I just focus in one direction, grab what I need and leave quickly, she thought to herself.

Sam continued to walk through the room as her eyes slowly adjusted. There was a small lamp plugged in by the doorway, but she didn't want to turn it on and see the spiders. Over time, she could start to see more things lying around the room over time. Old upturned stools, crates, and cardboard boxes that had unreadable scribbles on them.

Suddenly, one of the boxes caught her eye. It said "Violet" on it in black marker.

Sam took a moment, remembering the piece of paper she found in the dress pocket. She was contemplating taking a look inside. Why were these girl's things still here? Surely Miss Parr would not have wanted to hold onto them.

"I'll be quick," she muttered to herself. Sam hurried over to the box and pulled it down. There were cobwebs but, thankfully, no visible spiders or creepy crawlies.

Inside the box was a collection of soft toys, assorted bears, some still with tags on their ears. There were some loose playing cards defaced with crayon, a book about mermaids, and an empty glasses case.

Nothing exciting, which deflated Sam. She wasn't sure what to expect, but she expected more than this. She carefully placed the box back exactly how it was.

Reaching the back of the room, she still hadn't found the mop or the bucket. At this stage, she was retracing her steps. The room was divided by wine racks, so there were aisles to walk down. Many wine racks were empty, and the ones with bottles had not been touched in a long, long time.

Something brushed past Sam's leg. She saw and heard nothing — but it felt big.

Oh, Artemis? Remus? she thought to herself, though it was less comforting knowing either of the demon cats were prowling around her. Maybe it could smell a rat or something and had come down for breakfast. It was a thought she quickly wanted to forget. Spiders are one thing, but rats as well? No thank you.

After several minutes searching for the mop and bucket, Miss Parr's voice seemed to bounce through the darkness.

"Oh, I forgot, silly old me" there was a slight pause as Sam turned around towards the only source of light, being the entrance to the cellar.

"The mop and bucket are upstairs" she continued with an evil chuckle.

Sam was angry now at the purposeful and cruel trick she had played, and she wasted no time in leaving the wine cellar at all.

Miss Parr greeted Sam unpleasantly.. She was sitting at the table sipping on her tea. There was the mop and bucket sitting leaning against the table. Sam knew she was happy with herself and knew that she had no choice but to just mop the floor like a good child.

She filled the bucket with water, a grime had surfaced on it already and so she emptied it again and refilled it, she did this several times until there was no further scum on the top, luckily the mop head was untouched and so it was much easier to clean with this.

Sam was always doing chores like this when she was living with foster parents, at first she hated it but now it just passed the time. She used to daydream while doing this, imagining what she would eventually get to do with her life when she was old enough to start a family of her own.

That was what she wanted, she was thinking about it as she was methodically sweeping the wet mop across the old vinyl floor, only stopping to push the mop into the bucket to clean it off and continue. The water in the bucket had quickly turned from clear to a muddy grey colour and so she had to empty and refill the bucket again and again, it was tough work.

9

Not long after mopping the floor in the kitchen, Sam was sitting at the table and eating jam on toast, and like the stew she had the night before it was very tasty. Miss Parr for all her faults was a very good cook, but her portion sizes were small. Miss Parr was sitting just staring at Sam, her eyes wouldn't leave her, like a snake that was studying its prey and waiting for the opportunity to strike and sink in its venomous fangs. After finishing her breakfast, Sam looked up at Miss Parr, she didn't say anything but made it obvious she had finished.
"Now out of my sight, I have things to do"
Sam wasted no time on this instruction, she stood up and took her plate towards the sink, she picked up Miss Parr's empty plate as she passed. She said nothing in response, Sam for a moment was waiting on a thank you but then remembered her personality wouldn't ever emit such words like that.
After washing the plates and putting them away, Sam headed out of the kitchen leaving Miss Parr's presence who still said nothing as she left the room. Sam, heading back upstairs, continued down the corridor and came to a junction of corridors, feeling lost again. She stared down both routes and tried to remember, it felt like the entire house had shifted somehow.
A mere seconds later she decided that no matter which option

she chose, she would commit and explore anyway before heading back to her room and it just so happens she did actually decide on the wrong route back to her room after all. She came back to the junction in which she took the wrong turn the night before, she felt braver today after a night's sleep.

The sting on her ankle was still present, it felt like a hot needle piercing her skin, she worried about infection.

Sam decided to turn back to the kitchen and find something to aid the wound. Upon reaching the kitchen again, Artemis was sitting in the window and was now staring at her again, Miss Parr was not at the table anymore.

"Stop staring at me fleabag"

Artemis just stared back at her.

"What did you say, girl?!" Miss Parr was suddenly at the doorway and Sam felt a lump in her throat as she went a flushed bright red in her cheeks.

"Miss, Artemis swiped at my ankle last night, and I was just going to clean it up,"

Not making eye contact with Miss Parr in fear of her response, which was justified with Miss Parr's eyes becoming wide and angry.

Her spine went so straight it seemed to curve back in the wrong direction, she lifted her leg as she flung a pointed finger at Sam.

"LIES!"

She was screeching which caused a slight voice break, she lunged forward and grabbed Sam by the arm, she managed to close in the space between them in a split second. Gripping her forearm tighter and tighter she came close to Sam's face now, she could smell her putrid breath that stunk of rotten egg. Her voice then lowered to a wispy but more threatening tone. "Do you know what happens to children who lie?"

Now she was smiling, her eyes thinned, she was clearly enjoying this moment.

Sam said nothing, her head turned away from Miss Parr and was wincing.

Miss Parr pulled her out of the kitchen still grasping her arm, at first Sam's feet just slid across the floor before submitting and then began to follow obediently.

She tugged at her down the corridor, her hands so tight it was giving Sam a slight burning feeling underneath.

With one swing of her arm, Miss Parr flung Sam into a room and she landed on her elbow with a sharp knocking pain on the wooden floorboards, a dull pain and pins and needles shot up her arms into fingers as she had hit her funny bone.

"You will learn, or you will suffer the punishment, no more lies" Miss Parr stood in the doorway, now just a dark silhouette to the backdrop of a small amount of natural light behind her and with that moment she slammed the door shut and created the darkest blackness Sam had ever witnessed.

She fumbled around on her hands and knees, her hands scanning the floor around her as it was the only real sense that would assist her in the darkness. She realized her glasses had fallen off her face as she was flung to the ground. She placed them back on her face quickly; it was too dark to notice any

damage to the lenses.
Moments passed, and then she noticed it—a peculiar smell. It was stronger just a moment later. A bitter, floral scent—something like rotting lavender, if such a thing could exist. Sam pressed her face into the crook of her elbow, trying to block it out. It wasn't just unpleasant, it made her stomach twist.
A quiet shuffle echoed from somewhere in the room.
Sam froze.

She lifted her head just slightly, eyes straining in the pitch-black. There was no window, no light. Only that thin, unforgiving line beneath the door.
Another sound—a click. Soft. Rhythmic.

Tap.. Tap..Tap.

Just like the window the night before.

Her heart thudded so loud in her chest she was sure it was echoing off the walls. She wasn't imagining it. Something, someone, was in the room with her.
She wanted to scream, but her voice caught in her throat like it was stuck behind a wall of ice.

"Who's there?" she whispered, barely audible even to herself.

Nothing.

Then—a faint laugh. A child's laugh. So close it seemed to come from behind her own eyes.
Sam scrambled backward, her hands scraping against the gritty floorboards. Her back hit the wall.
The smell was thick now, coating her tongue. Her eyes darted around, searching for an answer.

Then she saw it.

A faint glow. Greenish. Sickly. Coming from a crack in the far wall, no bigger than a mousehole. She crawled toward it, desperate for answers, for anything to explain what was happening.
The glow pulsed.
And then a shadow moved across it. From the other side.
Sam gasped and stumbled back. Her heel caught on something and she fell, landing hard on her side.
That's when she saw them.
Eyes.
A pair of glowing, inhuman eyes blinking at her from the darkness—low to the ground, like they belonged to something crawling.

Then another pair. And another.

She wasn't alone in the room.

10

SIX MONTHS PREVIOUS..

Chris quickly filed his papers into his briefcase, sweat pouring down the side of his face. His jet-black hair, uncombed, stuck out in all directions, and his tie hung loose, barely committed to his shirt. *Late again*, he thought, brushing the sweat from his brow with his jacket sleeve. Only to realize that dark grey didn't hide it. Now there were just blotches of damp sweat across his arm.

He was an estate agent for *Clive's* in *Ilfracombe*, and there wasn't much competition. Clive himself, his boss, had once told him he had real promise, but he kept letting himself down with his timekeeping. And it wasn't something Chris could deny. He'd been up all night playing poker with his old squaddies. Since leaving the army, Chris's timekeeping had completely fallen apart.

At the time, he was working from his home office, which had become normal after the pandemic. His office was a jumble of loose papers, envelopes, coffee mugs, and books. He slammed the top drawer of his desk shut, realizing that a bunch of papers were stopping it from closing fully, but he just left them sticking out.

Chris used to live with his boyfriend Ryan, not that you'd

know he'd moved out. Their photos still cluttered every surface, smiling from frames like nothing had changed. They hadn't spoken in months. It wasn't that Chris hadn't moved on, he just hadn't gotten around to removing them yet. Frantically running down the stairs, his briefcase thudding against the bannister with each step, Chris fumbled to fasten his top button and tie, brushing his hair to the side with his fingers. He rushed out the front door, slamming it shut behind him, and sprinted onto the street where he lived, wedged between a dusty old DIY shop called *Drapers & Co* and a little record store named *Vinyl Revival*.

Clive's was only a few yards down the street, so Chris ran, already thinking of all the excuses he could use when he walked through the door. As he passed, blurred faces nodded or waved. *Ilfracombe* was the kind of town where everyone knew everyone.

There were few chain shops in town, which Chris liked. His friends called him an "old soul"

He preferred owning things physically, hated social media, and had never once streamed a movie without complaining. He burst through the office door.

"Sorry I'm late. Honestly, I'm so annoyed with myself," he said, slamming his briefcase onto the desk.

"We'll talk about that later," said Clive, one hand on his hip, glancing at the gold watch on his wrist.

"But aren't you supposed to be at the old zoo house, Chris?" Chris always thought Clive looked more like an archaeologist than an estate agent. Short, balding, and forever dressed in the same musty yellowish suit.

He reminded Chris of Belloq, Indiana Jones's rival in *Raiders of the Lost Ark*. His favourite movie of all time.

Muttering obscenities, Chris rushed back out the door. He yanked open the driver's side of his classic green MK1 Mini Cooper, tossed his briefcase onto the passenger seat, and climbed in. The engine sputtered like an old man having a coughing fit. He was already maneuvering from his parking spot before even fastening his seatbelt.

The little green Mini shuddered up the steep hill of *Oxford Grove* that connected the high street to the more residential area of the town. There were bin bags littering the streets, and children stopped with footballs and toys in hand, staring like the car had just landed from space. This was the roughest street in the whole town. Chris knew it well, having struggled to sell No. 38 for what seemed like two whole years.

Continuing through several streets and passing the local school, he arrived at what they called 'The Zoo House', named after the zoo that once stood where a holiday park now sat. It had lost funding back in the 1970s. The rumour was they let all the animals loose because it was the cheapest option, sparking the wild myth of the Ilfracombe black panther that people would debate in the Old Bell most nights.

"As big as an 'orse," he remembered one local fisherman saying.

The mansion sat across the road and had most likely housed staff or the owner of the zoo—maybe even functioned as a hotel.

As Chris drove into the car park, he noticed a tall, thin woman standing with her arms crossed. She looked angry, and Chris knew it was going to be a difficult sell. He parked the car swiftly and grabbed his briefcase as he opened the door.
"I am so sorry to keep you waiting—"
"Miss Parr," she snapped.
"Miss Parr! Great to meet you. I'm Chris Yates," he said, and they shook hands.
"Come inside. You are going to love this place. Is it just yourself?" Chris looked around, slightly confused as to why a lady on her own would be buying such a large house.
"Yes, just me and my cats."
Chris recoiled, he absolutely loathed cats.
"Well, this is the main hall. Great spacious area, of course. Leads here into a living room space, or maybe a library considering the bookcases built into the wall." Chris said, swiftly introducing some of the rooms. "Let me know if you have any questions. There's quite a lot of ground to cover on this property, so just stop me if you need anything," he explained.
Miss Parr said absolutely nothing throughout most of the tour. She just nodded at times when Chris gave suggestions for what could be done with some of the rooms, like, "This would be a perfect dining room space."
When they reached the third floor, Miss Parr abruptly snarled, "I'll take it."
Chris stopped in his tracks, stunned. He never expected this outcome—then remembered the commission he'd receive.

He smirked and turned around to shake her hand. Miss Parr glanced at it and ignored the gesture.

"Let's get the boring part out of the way. I would like to move in as soon as possible. Do you understand?" Miss Parr snapped, brushing her hands over the door frame, examining the dust. "It's not very clean, so I hope there will be some kind of discount."

"Well.. we dont really… I'll see what I can do." That was a lie, but there was no way he would be losing this sale. "There is, of course, some red tape to get through, but we'll do our best to hurry things along for you," Chris smiled politely.

Chris locked the mansion door behind them as Miss Parr walked out toward her old, black, beaten-up car. Chris couldn't figure out what it was she drove—it almost looked like a hearse.

"She's an old one!"

Chris shouted across the car park, pointing.

Miss Parr sarcastically smiled from the corner of her mouth and proceeded to get into the car.

What a miserable cow, he thought to himself. But no bother to him—he'd just sold the house.

11

After several attempts to start his car, Chris was finally able to pull away from the car park and back down the hill toward town. He now had his stereo on and was listening to a mixtape of 80s classics. By the time he approached *Oxford Grove* again, he was beating his hands on the steering wheel like drums to Union of the Snake by *Duran Duran*.

He parked in his usual spot outside Clive's. He couldn't park closer to home. The problem with Ilfracombe was the car parking was abysmal.

Entering through the glass double doors into the estate agents, which was a small area with royal blue carpets and light oak desks. Clive was deep in thought, his hand over his chin, as he rested with one leg on Suzie's desk.

"Guess who just sold the zoo house?" smirked Chris, as he again slammed his briefcase down onto his desk.

"Good work. Miss Parr stopped in 'ere this morning actually. Strange ol' fruitcake" Clive said, now shuffling through papers of new properties to list.

"I thought that too. Miserable old goat," laughed Chris, now lightly sitting on the end of his desk. He continued, "What on earth does a woman of her age, and all by herself, want with such a big house like that? She must be loaded though."

Chris noticed that Clive had lost attention and was now punching numbers into a calculator.
There was a slight pause in conversation and Clive disappeared into the kitchen, followed by the clanging of a spoon and cupboard doors. Suzie looked at Chris through her low-sitting glasses, chewing on what was probably the same piece of gum she'd had since yesterday.
"Sold it, did yer?" she said sarcastically.
"You were listening then? You continue to surprise me," Chris said with his back to her, now filling a small plastic cup with water from the cooler. Suzie was at least ten years older than Chris and was the nosiest and most annoying woman he'd ever had the misfortune to meet or work with. He was certain she was trying to have an affair with Clive for a promotion too.
Without warning, Clive was back in the room, stirring his mug of tea before Chris could even turn around.
 "Chris, we do need to talk about yer timekeeping," Clive said in a fairly concerned tone.
"I know, Clive, and there is no excuse. I'm sorry. I will continue to try an—"
 But Chris was cut off.
"You make these promises every time, an' we keep goin' in circles, Chris."
Clive sat down at his desk and took a sip from his tea.
"If it happens again within the next several weeks, t'will be a written warning, Chris. I have to draw the line somewhere, yer understand? You were in the army, kid. Yer should know

better."

He continued, now looking Chris in the eye to show he wasn't joking.

"I understand, Clive."

Chris sat down in his chair and snapped open the latches on his briefcase to pull out an apple.

It was the end of the working day, and Chris was slowly walking home down the same street he had felt like he was sprinting along just moments ago. This time, there were street lamps, as the night was drawing in fast. He sighed with relief as he reached his front door, exhausted. He reached into his pocket and pulled out his house keys. He discovered a small package had been squeezed through the letterbox.
Wrapped in green tissue paper, unwrapping it, a note dropped out: "Thank you for your help — this will bring you good luck. — Miss Parr," it read, scribbled in what looked like a fancy fountain pen.

He then pulled out a strange trinket. It was a bunch of sticks tied with string, forming a triangle. It creeped him out as it hummed with warmth in the palm of his hand, giving off its own energy. He wrapped it back up and placed it in the black wheelie bin outside the front door.

Chris flopped onto his sofa and turned on the TV. He glanced over at his shelf of Blu-ray movies, wondering what to pick. He had so many now that choosing a movie became a momentous task. He'd grab a movie, look at its cover from top to bottom, turn the box around and read the back. Sometimes even go to open the case only to change his mind and repeat the process four, five, maybe even six more times. But he eventually settled on *Gremlins*, because he hadn't seen it in so long. He opened the case, carefully took the disc out, and placed it inside his PlayStation. He didn't play video games; it was actually Ryan's, but he had never taken it with him when he left.

As the opening credits of the movie began, Chris was already asleep. This was a common occurrence on a weekday after work. he'd barely make it ten minutes on the sofa before he began to snore.
The power shut off completely in the house, and Chris remained asleep in darkness.

Minutes later, the doorbell rang out and echoed through the dark house. Chris woke with a shock. He hadn't expected to wake in complete darkness, and the temperature had dropped so dramatically that he could now see his breath.

He struggled to steady his breathing as the front door began banging loudly, as if someone were desperate to get in. He followed the hallway wall, never taking his eyes off the front door as he drew closer. There was no silhouette, but the door continued to bang every few seconds, and at one point, Chris feared it would come off its hinges, it was so violent.

As he got within reaching distance, Chris noticed he was sweating heavily. His ears began to ring so loud that he could no longer hear the banging in front of him. He realized he had never been so scared in his life. All the horror movies he'd watched up to this point couldn't compare, and he didn't even know what it was that terrified him so much.

He reached for the door handle and slowly opened it, hands trembling, heart pounding in his chest. He closed his eyes as he turned the knob, then peeked with one eye—

To his shock, there was no one there.
"Hello?" Chris stuttered, out of breath. He noticed the gift from earlier was now hanging in his porch. Even more freaked out, Chris walked backwards, not bothering to close the front door. He just stepped backward, breathing heavily, stunned by the sight of the trinket gently swaying left to right, tied to the porch's light fitting.

Chris ran to the sofa to grab his phone, which had fallen from his pocket. But he couldn't find it. It was just here. He wanted to call his friends to see if they were playing a prank on him. How could it just vanish? he thought, manically throwing the cushions from the sofa into the air.

Then he felt something brush the top of his head.

The room was full of trinkets, all dangling from the ceiling. At least fifty of them, all different shapes and sizes. Chris tried to scream, but he couldn't. Nothing escaped his lungs. Fear had completely gripped him.

He collapsed to the floor, vision spinning wildly. Pain tore through his chest, arms, and back—sharp and sudden, like a heart attack. Gritting his teeth, he dragged himself forward, each inch a battle as the room spiraled faster and faster around him.

Then came the heat, spreading across his back. And with it, a new pain. Not sharp. Not clean. It throbbed through

his bones like a toothache in every nerve.
 He reached behind him, desperate, and his fingers found something stuck there.

Something was wrong.

Warm blood coated his hands.

 His breath caught. Darkness closed in.

 And just before it swallowed him whole, he saw her face—Miss Parr, smiling softly.
"You shouldn't throw away gifts, Mr. Yates," she said.

 Then he was gone.

People gathered outside the house, watching as an ambulance carried away a body bag. Clive and Suzie watched in horror as their colleague was wheeled into the back. Clive had realised he was late that morning again and decided to go to his house, where he discovered the door was slightly open, and where he had discovered Chris' lifeless corpse.
Clive and Suzie sat at their desks in silence that morning. When the clock hit five past nine he lifted his mug to drink his tea. Only to realize it was empty.
Miss Parr walked in and lifted the keys from Chris' vacant desk.
    "These are mine, I believe?" she smiled.

Clive looked at her, his weakened mind gave into a trance state. He offered a fake half-smile and waved her away with his free hand.

"Excellent. My cats will be so happy.

12

PRESENT DAY

"Hush, little baby, don't say a word. Mama's going to buy you a mockingbird."

A voice crawled out of the darkness towards Sam, her eyes fixed on the corner of the room, but she couldn't see anything. She knew it wasn't Mrs. Thompson. This voice was too wispy-sounding and too malevolent. The voice continued to sing, becoming more breath-filled, like the last words of a dying child. Sam realised it was a child's voice.
"Who's there? I can't see you!"
Sam called out. Her voice didn't stop, it kept ricocheting through the darkness like it had a mind of its own, twisting and warping until it no longer sounded like her at all. It was now starting to feel like a nightmare that she couldn't awaken from.
Then it happened, the most terrifying thing Sam had ever witnessed.
It began with a gust of wind, sharp and sudden, slapping cold against her face. She froze. A door groaned open, the sound long and splintered, like wood dragging across bone.
Then came a noise, something being pulled. Not once, but again. And again. Each dragging sound stuttered in its own

time, like they weren't coming from the same room. Like they weren't coming from the same now. Her eyes darted to a lamp on the wall, with a pull chord. With shaking fingers, she pulled at it with a click.

Eyes.

From the low lit end of the room, plastic fingers clicked onto the floor, one after another, as the dolls emerged. Mrs. Parr's dolls, impossibly animate, crawled forward. soft light catching the shine of their glassy skin and frozen smiles.
They moved in a slow, broken rhythm. Some dragged their limbs like they had forgotten how to use them. Some twitched with too much life, scrambling forward as if desperate to reach her first.

They were singing.

High-pitched voices, off-key and too sweet, spilled from their mouths.

Some giggled like babies.

Some cried out in fractured, mechanical tones: "Mummy…"

Sam felt her heart rising through her chest and into her throat, terrified. She had all of a sudden realised that hands were also around her ankles and the jet black eyes were staring from directly below, she finally managed to scream and it was a blood curdling scream that echoed through the halls of the house.

The door unlocked and swung open, and Miss Parr's silhouette now filled the space.

"What on earth is all this commotion?" Miss Parr was furious that such a sound had fluttered through her normally very quiet house. Sam realised the dolls were back in their normal homes behind glass doors in the cabinets.

"It was the dolls Miss, the dolls were crawling to me" Sam was in tears now and fell to her knees, she was emotionally exhausted after what had just happened.

"Childish girl, what do you take me for? Do you think I am stupid, do you have something wrong with your silly little brain?' Miss Parr's face seemed to stretch out with her wild expression, almost mimicking what Sam was feeling which was indeed completely mad.

Sam had now questioned her entire experience and felt like she was in a dream state, like she wasn't real and she was floating outside of her body and it's not something she has never felt before either as she pinched the skin of her arm to understand she was real and what she witnessed was seemingly real too.

"Off to bed with you now, I've had enough of you today" Miss Parr turned up her nose again as she spun on her heel, this time her ankles clicked and popped grotesquely.

She shut the door behind her as she left the room, feeling the eyes still watching her every move. She heard a small giggle from one of the cabinets before she could exit, but she dismissed it, too tired to continue being terrified.

Laying in bed for several hours, she couldn't sleep at all or even keep her eyes closed as the moonlight shone through the small window and beamed off the wall. She was replaying the events that occurred earlier over and over again in her mind and tried to come up with an explanation. *Have I lost my mind? Did it actually happen? Is this place haunted?*

 Sam, despite being terrified of the house, had never believed in ghosts. She had never seen or felt one and had never been visited by the people she would expect to visit her from beyond the grave.

Her mouth parched after all that had happened, feeling like all the emotion had dehydrated her, but terrified to go and get a glass of water.

She imagined not only waking up Miss Parr to be utterly terrifying, but also having to navigate most of the house in the dark.

Several minutes passed by and after much internal debate she climbed out of bed and slowly crept towards the bedroom door, her heart was already racing as she carefully tiptoed across the dusty wooden floorboard as she tried to remember which ones were creaky. She reached for the door handle and slowly turned it, realizing how loud just this action made her pause, it was one of those round door handles that seemed to rattle the entire door just turning it slightly. Sam then placed her hand firmly on the door as she turned the knob and pulled the door too, giving it more stability and helped ease the sounds of the creaking wood. Beyond the door was the staircase that led to the third floor and it was in complete blackness.

Taking her first step through her bedroom door, she realised she was holding her breath just doing this. She let herself breathe and focused for a second on that to calm her down. She took further steps using her hand to guide herself along the handrail to ensure she didn't fall over, she was terrified of missing a step and taking a tumble down. which would for certain wake up Miss Parr from her slumber.

Counting the steps for future reference until reaching the bottom of the staircase. Turning to her right, she stared down into the black abyss, the corridor with its closed doors on both sides.

Sam slowly began walking through, it was hard to keep her footing because it was so dark she couldn't see her hand in front of her face.

Her hand brushed the wall to her left as a guide, occasionally losing touch of it as she came to the next doorway. She noticed that walking past one of the doors she could hear the wind through the bottom of the door and felt a nasty cold just dance around her toes. It seemed to penetrate her skin and freeze her very bones.

Eventually reaching a dead end, realizing there was a left turn. She was greeted with another long, dark corridor, with no doors on either side, but she could make out the shape of a large potted house plant to the right in the middle.

Increasing pace now and reaching the stairs down to the next floor. This journey seemed to be so much longer than it should have been. The darkness stretched the layout of the house, confusing Sam and distorting her memory. She walked down the stairs slowly which were much more sturdy and less noisy with carpet running down the centre of them.

As she reached the bottom of the stairs and onto the second floor. She heard shuffling behind her, it wasn't Artemis, it was too large to be him.

She brushed off the noise and continued to head on to the kitchen. Sam navigated the endless halls of doors that were open this time around but there was nothing of significance in them that she could tell, occasionally sticking her in the doorways to glance around, as she reached the staircase to the first floor, Remus was there on the bottom step with his back to Sam, like a guard, his eyes fixed on the door that led into another corridor.

Sam had really grown to hate this cat ever since she arrived only a few days ago.

It was short haired and completely grey, making it easier to spot in the darkness than Artemis, its piercing glowing eyes almost hypnotising you before it hisses and reveals its crooked fangs.

Reaching the bottom step, Remus gave a low and deep growl which sent all the hairs on the back of her neck standing to attention, cold beads of sweat began to form on her brow and all of her exposed skin felt like it was experiencing an extreme case of pins of needles. "Pssst! Shoo!" Sam had whispered this but also with another volume to show authority to Remus, who just looked up at her with a demonic stare as his eyes thinned.

Sam was happy to get through the door and closed it firmly behind her and was happy knowing Remus had not followed. Sam curiously opened the door wide enough to peek through and saw that Remus was still sitting there just staring at her like it could see straight through the door. Sam shut the door and stood facing the dark corridor ahead, she stood for a moment composing herself.

Sam reached the Kitchen which was less pitch black than the rest of the house, its window let in the moonlight that was directly facing and cast shadows against the kitchen work tops and bounced off various antique like plates and mugs, that old blue and white china that every grandmother seemed to possess but never actually use. No crumbs remained from the afternoon bread, and no rings marked the surface from the tea Miss Parr seemed to constantly consume. Someone placed everything perfectly and kept it spotless.

Sam began to slowly and quietly open some of the doors, not knowing where the glasses were kept.

Sam quietly poured herself a glass of water after finding the correct cupboard and she was making sure that the water was only slightly dripping from the tap to avoid too much noise. Lifting the glass to her parched lips, a loud, sharp banging noise came from below. She felt it under her feet and remembered that Miss Parr's section of the ground floor had very large and heavy-looking wooden doors. She was convinced it was those that just slammed, and now began to panic that Miss Parr was about to catch her.

Still clutching the now half full glass, had now gotten onto her hands and knees and shuffled quickly under the small table that had a table cloth neatly laid over it, this gave her some cover and she could see the entire room from here.

Swallowing hard as she heard footsteps coming up the stairs. She was startled by the noise, and she panicked, fearing Miss Parr knew she was there.

Feet became visible in the doorway.

Still for a moment, while Sam noticed she had a hooded robe on. It was definitely the same height as Miss Parr but there were no recognisable features in the dark. It seemed to glide across the kitchen towards the window. The moonlight revealed her crooked, misshapen nose. More detail on her bare feet revealed that the toe nails were long, misshapen, miss-coloured and looked like they had been walking for days as they were scratched and had damaged skin all over.

Placing her hand over her mouth, she felt sick from this sight. She was conscious her breathing was louder with the panic. She could hear Miss Parr's breathing now and noticed it was steaming up a small section of glass on the window she was facing. It was a weak shallow breath but almost wispy and ghost-like.

She then began to whisper in a language that Sam couldn't recognise. "Ubi est puella?"

The figure turned again towards the door and with quicker pace and heavier footing, stormed out the room and shut the door.
With a heavy sigh of relief Sam's entire body relaxed, slowly climbed out from under the table to a standing position and finished her glass of now room temperature water. She carefully washed the glasses and polished it with a tea towel, ensuring no marks or smudges were on the glass, again she began to imagine, this time Miss Parr inspecting everything in the kitchen for fingerprints.
Sam slipped the glass back in the cupboard, ensuring it looked untouched. Quietly creeping towards the door and opening it enough to peek through and check Miss Parr wasn't waiting for her on the other side. Met instead with a dark corridor, she looked down towards the ground floor. The stairway was clear, it was deafeningly quiet again.
She quickly paced back to her room, feeling certain Remus would be waiting for her to appear so he could lunge again. Unfortunately this also meant passing the room she was in earlier, the room which contained those dolls.
The door to the room was wide open.
Walking past she heard it again, the childish giggle. Sam just decided to run and everything blurred around her. She held her hands out to guide her through the dark. Feeling like those dolls were now chasing her, but when turning her head there was nothing but black.
She had reached her bedroom and slammed shut the door behind her, not caring now what noise she had made, not

caring about what Miss Parr could hear. She was terrified of the noise she had just heard from those dolls again. *What was happening? Was it a demon in the house possessing them? Or was it Miss Parr? Was it Artemis or Remus*? Such silly thoughts ran through her head but she knew what she had heard and there was no denying it.

Climbing into bed and pulling the sheets over her head, Sam closed her eyes and focused on the breathing, she counted to four in between breathing in, holding it and breathing out. It made her mind sharper doing this, it cleared the crazy thoughts that began to flood her just a moment ago.

She continued to focus on breathing and her eyes began to become heavy. She felt relatively safe in her room now as she had spent so much time there over the last few days cowering under her sheets.

Sam had become aware that she was half awake, she was stirring and it was unlike her to do this, she is normally a heavy sleeper and was always happy that this was the case. Frightened to look outside of the sheets. She realized it was still late at night, and horrific thoughts filled her mind that her room was now infested with those dolls.

She screamed from the top of her lungs as her sheets were pulled from the bed and flung into the air, accompanied by a wispy ghostly groaning sound.

Sam was frozen solid, there was no one else in the room and the sheet was now on the other side of it next to the old wardrobe.. In the moment Sam had retreated her knees to her chest and was now curled up tight, only looking at the room with the movement of her eyes under her fringe, she just couldn't move a muscle in her body, now she had closed her eyes and began to focus on breathing and focusing on undoing the tension all over her body.

Gathering enough courage, Sam walked over to the light switch to illuminate the room, she walked over to the bedsheets and dragged them behind her as she walked back to the bed. Sam slept only a short amount of time for the rest of the night and had the bedroom remaining illuminated

13

Birds chirped from the window ledge outside, and for an autumn morning it was particularly sunny. Sam stirred, awakening from a deep sleep that had been disturbed by the many events of the previous night.. When she opened her eyes, the light made them ache. She wished she had a few more hours before she had to wake, and she had to ensure she was dressed, so the light that was left on would be off when Miss Parr arrived.
Sam climbed from the bed rubbing her eyes and stretching out her arms, one of those big stretches that makes you feel dizzy for just a moment.
She realized she was still fully clothed, reaching for the light switch.
Folding her clothes neatly she placed them inside the ottoman. She didn't want to touch the wardrobe. Though the cherub faces looked a lot more innocent during the day compared to the evil soul absorbing stare they gave her in the dead of night. She paired her socks, thinking to herself that today was probably the day she would be forced to use some kind of old Victorian device to wash her clothes.
The door swung up and Miss Parr barged in with a long piece of rolled up paper, it was very old looking and almost

resembled parchment that Sam had seen in old movies.

"You will go into town today and fetch me these things that I have written down. They must be these things exactly and I expect you to not mess around, do not go off course and finish the task in good time, do you understand girl?"

Miss Parr rolled her words like a snake again, her face seemed more defined in the sunlight, her eyes sunken in but Sam recognised the crooked nose from last night in the moonlight of the kitchen.

It was definitely her.

"Excuse me miss, but i am not sure how to get to town from here" Sam explained with her hands held together in front of her politely. 'I'm not going to let you get there on your own, I will be close by, I must go and do something important while you fetch me my things" she sneered and had a hint of sarcasm in her tone.

Sam didn't like the idea of her having to walk down into town with Miss Parr by her side, she was more concerned about the lack of conversation and awkward silence.

The two of them headed downstairs into the main lobby area, the house was a lot brighter, you could make out the paintings on the walls which were mostly cats, and scenic woodland paintings but also some strange creatures that Sam didn't recognise.

They reached the main reception room and slipped on coats, the one handed to Sam was slightly too big but she was just happy to have a coat on. They headed out the big wooden front doors that Miss Parr had to really push to open them and lost her footing slightly in doing so.

Relieved to be outside in the fresh air for the first time in days, as she stepped out into the gravel car park. She was hoping that this would take a good while to get into town and get the shopping list complete and back home again and this would be a good distraction to what had happened the night before that had terrified her.

They walked out onto the main road, to the left was the holiday park that overlooked a huge portion of the town and just next to that sat a little quaint bungalow, one that Sam thought was delightful and thought it was a good distance that someone might be able to help if she needed it.

Straight ahead was a school and its football field, while it was a functioning secondary school it also looked like a factory, it had a great chimney in the middle of the compound that reminded her of some kind of Nazi concentration camp.

"Excuse me miss, but will I go to school here when term starts again?" Miss Parr was looming over Sam like an evil spirit. "School? Hah. You're lucky I didn't lock you in the attic. I told them I'd homeschool you." she smiled with a sarcastic tone from the side of her mouth and her eyebrows lifting high. At this moment it dawned on her that she wouldn't get any kind of education.

Miss Parr, noticing how sad Sam was looking at that moment, decided to relish in this with an evil cackle "You think I'm a monster don't you?" Miss Parr put her hand on Sam's shoulder which caused her to recoil, like a turtle retreating into its shell.

Sam paused before continuing the peace with a stuttering voice "No Miss" and then Sam continued to walk down the road, they walked past the school which now that they were closer, Sam could look in through the windows and get a glimpse of what the classrooms looked like, being nearly Halloween and half term the school was eerily quiet.

They continued walking down the road, they had come to a steep hill and a roundabout that led in several directions but mostly led to more houses. Outside one of these houses sat an old man with a cigarette dangling from his mouth and a newspaper on his lap. He must have been in his eighty's. She always struggled to guess ages correctly. He spotted them both walking past and waved his hand in the air.

"Keep walking Girl"

Miss Parr said like a ventriloquist dummy she barely moved her mouth and didn't even acknowledge the friendly old man. They were now at the bottom of the steep bend which revealed taller houses on either side of the road, with cars parked all the way down, ahead you could see hills with a few large houses dotted around but mostly concealed by tall trees.

It was at this moment Sam realised how pretty the town actually was and could only imagine what the seafront would be like as she imagined a great sandy beach and crashing waves.

They continued past a church on the left, Sam paused. The gravestones leaned like trees after a storm, their names long erased.

Making a sharp right turn they were on *Oxford Grove*, a street that Sam remembers seeing before, it seemed almost endless but you could see the high street at the bottom which looked like a miniature model from where they were standing.

The sun beamed off the houses at the bottom of the road which made the atmosphere feel like it was the middle of summer, you wouldn't believe that it was nearly halloween if if it wasn't for the dried dead leaves all over the pavement and bunched by the sides of roads.

There were even a few pumpkins dotted around on garden walls and kitchen windows.

They continued down the steep hill, this was a very gross looking area to live in. It had bin bags piled up nearly taller than Sam on the side of the pavement, you could smell all kinds of old food and sometimes a sweet but grotesque smell that she was sure to be drugs of some kind.

There was a smashed in door that they had passed with debris all over the carpet inside, it seemed like it was most likely a raid by the police.

The atmosphere quickly changed as they reached the high street though, with a row of shops either side of the street, the traffic was steady, not heavy by any stretch of the imagination like Sam had witnessed in other towns but there were still a lot of people around.

They walked past a cinema which had clearly been letting people out of a screening, this was the first instance that Sam had seen younger people and they were all smiling and some holding hands.

Sam was feeling a little anxious now, it was the first time she had felt like she was amongst civilisation for a long time. Miss Parr grabbed her arm and forced the paper list into her hand. "Right, you'll find most of these items in that shop over there" she pointed at a herbal remedy type of shop, it wasn't a chain that she could tell, it looked like a small local place. "Don't chit chat, i will meet you back here in forty five minutes understood?"

Sam was daydreaming while staring around at the tall buildings, most of the shops had several floors of flats above them. "Answer when you are spoken to" Miss Parr snapped and hit her round the back of the head with her leather gloves. "Yes Miss" even though she was barely listening she just nodded and before she realised she was gone, Miss Parr's tall bony structure was half way up the street already and vanishing from view.

She was distracted by anything that was moving as she shuffled across the street towards the shop.

An old woman with a trolley and her back curved over stopped and smiled at her. "Hello dear" she said. "Hello" Sam replied with a smile, it was nice to know that there were still good people in the world.

Arriving in front of the shop that she was directed to. It was painted with green and gold branding, ivy leaves dangling down from above the shop window. Above the door spelled The Healing Hole and there were flowers dotted around. Sam loved how peaceful it seemed inside and pushed the door open, the bell above it ringing out to signal a customer. Another old lady was at the till, she looked quite hagged and clearly was knocking on death's door, she had a dark scarf around her head with no hair on show and she was wearing a large dark brown fur coat. Hunched over the counter in front of what looked like Tarot cards and quietly muttering to herself.

Sam could not make out what it was she was saying but she slowly looked up and stared at Sam, it was an unnerving stare and revealed that the woman had a left black glass eye.

She smiled revealing not many teeth at all, and the ones left were in the middle and browning.

"Hello dear" what followed was a nasty hacking cough of someone who had smoked a hundred cigarettes.

"Um.. Hi" Sam replied anxiously, putting her hand up to wave and the old woman continued to look down at the cards and mutter to herself.

Unfolding the list, now slightly damp with the anxious sweat of her palm.

- White Peppers
- Black Salt
- Oak Tree Bark
- Lavender Incense
- Vanilla Root Beans
- Honey Stones

These items seemed so peculiar, like something out of a fantasy story with Elves and Dragons. Sam even slightly giggled to herself at the silliness of it.

"What yer got there?"
The old lady followed with a slight cough.
Sam walked over to the counter and the old woman with a swipe of her hand moved her Tarot cards to the side. Placing the list on the counter nervously, and now she could smell the old woman. It was putrid and didn't smell that different to the bin bags that littered the street earlier on the walk to town.
"Interesting, I assume this list is for Florence?"
The old lady was using a magnifying glass attached to a chain around her neck to read the list. The revelation that Miss Parr's first name was Florence.
 "Miss Parr,"
There was a pause.
"thought so" with a wheezey cackle.
The old lady slid around the shop like a wounded animal. Crouched over with a rather large hump on her shoulder, that seemed to be weighing her down.
Sam realised how she didn't quite look human at all in some ways. She revealed her badly burnt hands.
The old lady grabbed things in quick succession from the shelves and into a bag.
"Been ere for 60 years, this shop belonged to my mother yer know" Sam just listened and slowly followed her around the shop that was overflowing with all kinds of bottles, crystals, flowers, bags of petals and all sorts of strange trinkets.
"So you know Miss Parr?"
Sam now gaining confidence to try and gather some knowledge.

"Everyone around ere knows ol' Florence"
The old woman was spitting as she talked now, with drips landing on some of the shelving aside them and masking amongst the black painted pinecones that sat in a pile.
"Who on earth would want to buy a black painted pinecone?" Sam said realising she was thinking out loud and then panic set in as she had to catch her next breath.
The old woman stopped and stared at Sam before quickly continuing to gather items on the list and then shoving the bag in her hands. "Thirty five pounds eighty two pence please" she snarled as Sam counted the money given to her and handed it over. Sam wasted no time leaving the shop.
"Bloody youngsters, think they know it all now, they know now't"

14

1940

Florence awoke to the sound of birdsong—an unfamiliar chorus compared to the muffled silence of winter nights in London, 1940.

The bombings had driven her and her sister, Mary, from the city to the coastal town of Ilfracombe. Their mother was dead, lost to Tuberculosis the year before, and their father was somewhere in Europe, swallowed up by the war. Letters had stopped coming. Their aunt in London had quietly confessed that she doubted he was ever coming home.

Florence was upset and reflected from the events of the day before, they had just arrived in Ilfracombe by train and a bunch of the other evacuated children on the train were being nasty to her. They were teasing her about being ugly and taller than average for her age. There was no division of class on the train, Florence was stuck with some of the richest children in London in the same carriage.

Florence and her sister grew up in a fairly poor household. Her father did not work, and for a long while he was on the run from being drafted in the war.

Her mother was a hairdresser, but business had begun to suffer when the war broke out and the gents had all shipped off.

The girls were placed with a peculiar family in a strange town.

Living in a large mansion that sat opposite the local zoo. It seemed to be struggling financially as there were never crowds or queues of people wanting to get a glimpse of the animals.

Walking down to the dining room for breakfast the next morning, she followed the smell of toast and fresh orange juice.

"And what time do you call this?"

It was Mr Fawnes, a thin, well dressed man. He was a chief inspector of the Devonshire police force; he didn't have to wear a police uniform. He wore a suit and it was immaculate. Not a speck on him out of place, his round glasses perfectly aligned on his face. With frustrated eyes he peered out of them. A well trimmed, and oiled Mustache completed his image.

"City kids. Should've shoved them in a factory, not someone's home," he muttered, scribbling his crossword.

Sat opposite was a small framed woman, she seemed quite nervous around her husband, she said nothing as she quietly watched her small children eat their toast. They had two twin children, Tommy & Riley. Florence was quite fond of them, they were cheeky.

"May I have some more orange juice please?" Asked Mary.

"Of course dear"

Mrs Fawnes raised the jug and began to pour Mary a fresh glass. Mr Fawnes was furious now over this and slammed down the glass while still in Mary's grasp, his palm remained cusping it down to the table with some strength.

"No Elizabeth, what do you think this is? They must earn it, they must do chores, they must help around the house and around the town to earn their right to be here. They send them to our town in the hundreds expecting everyone to just welcome them in, these are complete strangers and for all we know they could be bloody Nazi children themselves!"

Mr Fawnes red faced and eyes bloodshot, as he went off on a rant. His wife said nothing, but it didn't stop him from continuing as he stormed off to work. He slammed the wooden front doors behind him.

Florence blinked rapidly, willing the tears not to fall. Her stomach clenched—shouted words always curled around her like old ghosts. She had enough of that back at home with her own parents. And even though she missed them dearly, it felt like nothing had changed as it was so familiar.

After a brief silence at the breakfast table, both Florence and Mary headed upstairs and after a few hours had passed playing games and colouring in pictures of various animals. Florence and her sister Mary were playing in one of the unused rooms, it was a big empty room on the third floor with two very large windows overlooking the front of the house and car park.

They danced and jumped around without the risk of breaking anything valuable in the house and made animal impressions and funny impressions of people they knew back home. Like Martin, the strange man who lived next door to them, he had a stutter that always made them laugh and they would try to make him say funny things to encourage it.

They were taking turns blindfolding each other and spinning

around, they would have to find the other person while dizzy. It was a game they would play all the time as it didn't require anything and it was always hilarious to watch the other person stumble around.

Florence wrapped her scarf around Mary's head, tightly so she couldn't cheat. Counting to ten as she spun Mary around on the spot. They were both chuckling and as Florence reached ten, she backed away quickly and hid in the corner of the room.

Mary stumbled around, her arms were front reaching as she tried to feel anything familiar to find her sister and win the game. They used to love this game at home but they were always breaking things because the house was too small, this room alone for them was perfect for it.

Unfortunately this memory for Florence would haunt her, it would shape her and change her forever. It all happened so quickly, before Florence could grab her Mary tripped over her own feet and slammed into the glass pane of the window, Florence saw it all happen in slow motion. With an almighty crashing of glass and the sound of shards hitting the wooden floor Mary began to tumble head first over the windowsill and out of sight. Florence screamed from the top of her lungs and rushed to the window, it was as if she was in a nightmare, she would often have nightmares about the floor becoming a tar like substance that she couldn't move in and it felt exactly like this.

She saw her younger sister's lifeless body lying on the gravel car park, there was blood pooled around her head as it began to spread and trickle out further, trickling its way to finding a path amongst the stones.

Florence's scream tore through the house. She dropped to her knees, clutching the windowsill until her knuckles turned white. The world wavered behind a veil of tears.

Mrs Fawnes rushed out onto the gravel and fell down at Mary's lifeless body, her hands clutched her arms but didn't know what to do in the panic. A car on the main road had stopped and a man had run out leaving the car door open and in the middle of the road to help.

Florence remained at the broken window, she felt like her world had collapsed around her and that all meaning to her life had ceased to exist, her sister was everything to her and she couldn't imagine life without her as she uncontrollably sobbed.

For the next hour, people at the house took photos. There were police questioning Florence and Mrs Fawnes. Even Mr Fawnes had to get involved with the case. He scowled at Florence from across the room, and with that she was certain that he thought she had murdered her.

She couldn't talk for days after this event, it turned into weeks before she uttered just a few small words to the family at the table over breakfast, lunch or dinner. She rarely ate, she lost excessive amounts of weight and seemed to never sleep.

The kids who lived nearby would call her names, they would accuse her of killing Mary and pushing her out the window in a jealous rage for attention. Kids would knock at the door and run away as they shouted "Murderer" "Freak" or "Psycho" as they ran off down the road.

Becoming more withdrawn, she would often go down to the beachfront to try and get away from everything. She came back with a black eye on occasion or a split lip as someone in the town had decided to hit her for being a "Freak orphan girl" Florence had sunk into reading books, it was an escapism for her but it became an unhealthy obsession as he began reading up on odd subjects, she tried to learn how to place a witch's curse on the local bullies, it failed of course but, it didn't stop her from trying very hard to be successful.

As time went on in the house and the war raged on, Florence had started to dress differently, she discarded all her childish clothes and had sewn and fashioned her own dresses, mostly dark blues and blacks. But her new obsession was frightening to the family.

One day when Florence was aimlessly walking around the high street, she found herself in a small side street where she met a very curious old lady.

This woman had encouraged Florence to approach her and that she had some great things to show her, she had great knowledge of dark spells, curses and the power of herbal alchemy. The old lady seemed to know far too much about Florence's past, like it was a film just released and she had studied. Florence would often go to meet her to console, it seemed this strange nameless woman was the only soul that was willing to listen.

During their meeting the woman handed her a book some days later. Handwritten many many centuries ago by a local witch.

It held instructions on how to resurrect a loved one from the dead.
When Mrs Fawnes would go shopping for groceries, Florence would make requests for the strangest of items, Mrs Fawnes never brought them back and so Florence would have to go looking for local plantlife, but would sometimes go and steal what she needed.
Mr Fawnes had even bailed her out of the local police station for stealing on multiple occasions.

A year had passed and Florence was no closer to actually resurrecting her sister. This was obvious, she was a young girl and was reading about spells that seemed to come out of a fairytale, talking about all these crazy ingredients she had never heard of before.
 She was severely depressed and was running out of patience. She began to take her frustration out on small animals like Rabbits and Squirrels in the woods close by to the house. It started by accident when she would go out into the woods and throw stones at the trees, screaming at them and crying, she would scream things like "Bring me back my Sister, if there is a god, where is he? Why has he abandoned me?" one of the stones she threw had hit a squirrel out of a tree and killed it instantly. Something in her twisted at the sight of its stillness. Not guilt. Not horror. Just... relief. And that scared her most of all.. This was alarming to Mr & Mrs Fawnes who decided enough was enough, they were going to send her away to another family.

However this plan never came to fruition, on Christmas Eve of 1940 shortly after the children went to bed to expect Father Christmas the next morning. The house caught alight at around three in the morning.

Florence was rushed to the hospital with smoke inhalation, but the rest of the family had perished. Both Mr & Mrs Fawnes had both burned alive trying to fight through the flames to get to their children on the next floor. The Children died by the toxic smoke that quickly filled their rooms while they slept. Florence was questioned time and time again during the investigation that had followed. There were questions about how she was able to survive. She slept in the attic room of the house, and yet she was able to make it through three floors of a raging inferno. The ceilings had mostly collapsed, and left so many routes out of the house unpassable. But it was never revealed how she escaped.

Investigators couldn't find the cause of the fire and suspected it was an electrical problem, so they closed the case. There seemed to be a few fires in the town due to the age of the buildings and the shabby electrical work within them. There was a large hotel on the front that once caught fire and nearly took half the town with it.

Moving from house to house over the next few months, Florence was able to go home back to London to live with her aunt eventually. She had to endure further German bombings over the city, but they began to become few and far between as the focus shifted on the northern cities.

Her aunt told her that her father had been killed when they

were trying to take back a small French town from the Germans.

Feeling numb to this news, Florence spent her days reading books in her bedroom. She had seemingly lost all emotional response and then she laughed uncontrollably in the face of her aunt. She was absolutely mortified.

Her aunt was becoming increasingly scared of Florence, her personality had drastically changed on returning to London. She was angry all the time, she wouldn't go out and play with children her own age, she would draw strange and terrifying symbols on her bedroom walls in red crayon. And she was always hungry, her hunger was never fulfilled.

Her aunt, convinced Florence had become possessed by an evil entity, even tried to get a local priest to perform a Christian ceremony to banish the spirits.

Her aunt would often come face to face with her brother's decayed corpse standing in the living room, still in his military uniform but with half of his face blown off. Revealing broken tissue, torn muscle and a loose eyeball. He would stand to attention before vanishing into thin air.

Pets in the local area started to go missing not long after this started happening. Florence's aunt found a small box under Florence's bed that had teeth, dog hair, cat hair, photos, and bloody collars stashed in it.

Florence would be sent to a boarding school after this, it was a strict catholic school where she would hurl things at the teachers. She would scream obscenities, sometimes pretending she had become possessed by some demon.

Miss Glockworth, one of the teachers at school, was concerned for Florence. She was always trying to help kids that were in trouble. Having been abused in many ways, they would come through the door and she would often dig deeper, and try to help.

Mocking her good nature, Florence called her all the obscenities one can imagine, and spread rumours about her not being a true christian. She'd spread lies about her having sexual encounters with men on a nightly occurrence. Which wasn't true of course, but Florence twisted the knife so much that she was let go after eight years of working for them. Eventually her behaviour seemed to spread like a disease, the other children would act up and begin to mimic her behaviour.

15

PRESENT DAY

With a ring of the bell, the shop door closed behind her. Sam exhaled deeply, clutching the green-and-gold plastic bag tighter as she stepped into the open air. The bag in her hand was sagging due to the weight and she didn't look forward to having to carry it all the way back to the house. The air was so fresh in her lungs as she focused on her breathing, she could smell the salt air and she longed to see the beachfront, hidden behind shops and townhouses. If she listened carefully, she could hear the waves and the distant cries of gulls.

Slowly and reluctantly Sam walked back to the meeting point, she wished she could just run but she had nowhere to go. She stopped at most of the shop entrances to smell some of the nicer things, there was a perfume shop that had a strong rose scent that danced around Sam's nostrils and a chocolate shop that smelt so rich and she could practically taste it. Sam had rarely eaten chocolate in her life.

Sam stopped at the edge of the pavement and looked both ways before crossing, she was a smart girl that knew what danger was. After all her best friend back at the Orphanage, Christie, who was only a few years younger than Sam, had stepped out in front of an oncoming white van that was going way past the speed limit. It took her down and she died instantly, splitting her head on the road and leaving a nasty scene. Some say she was trying to escape from her carers but sometimes bad things happen to good people.

She crossed the road and could see Miss Parr leaning against a lamppost, she looked like she was impatient. As she got closer, a man with two great German Shepherds had walked past Miss Parr and they suddenly went wild with anger, their whole demeanor changed like they were leaders of a pack and they were in danger. They snarled at Miss Parr and the owner had trouble keeping hold of the leashes. These dogs were foaming at the mouth and barking excessively, they were chomping their fangs to get at her.

"I am so sorry miss, I don't know what's come over them"

The man, although small in stature and very thin, had a very surprising strong grip, it's most likely because he knew her life depended on that grip of his.

"Get your beastly things away from me man, If I had my way, I'd have them put down"

Miss Parr was equally foaming at the mouth now, her eyes wider than Sam had ever seen them before and she looked almost cartoon like.

The man looked terrified and ashamed, his head bowed in submission and with that hurried his dogs along and out of sight.

Both Sam and Miss Parr were now walking back towards the sloped run down street of *Oxford Grove*.

When they finally reached the top, Sam's calf muscles were strained. It was tough to get to the top of the steep road. Miss Parr wasn't struggling at all. For her age she should have been only half way up by now, but showed no signs of slowing down.

They had now come to the steep sloped and forked road where the old man was sitting outside of his bungalow, he was no longer there but the chair and the newspaper remained.

On the walk back, they passed the school, which was opposite large sloped fields. The horses were hanging their heads over the small barbed fence and Sam thought they must have been waiting for food. Perhaps the school kids would come out after the bell and feed them.

Stopping to stroke the mane of one of the horses, Sam was in absolute awe at this moment, like all her problems had gone away and Sam very much loved horses, she had only really seen them in books but did once ride a horse and ever since became fascinated by them. Perhaps it was the freedom that they possessed or represented. The dark grey and beautifully groomed horse did not put up a fight against Sam's palm but with one glance and direct eye contact with Miss Parr and the Horse suddenly bolted, in fact the other three had also already bolted.

What was it with her? Why were animals so terrified of her? Sam thought to herself, bewildered by this second occurrence in a matter of hours.

"Hurry up Girl" snapped Miss Parr as she clicked her fingers pointing to an empty space beside her.

Saying nothing in response, Sam bowed her head just like the man with the dogs did, complete submission. What choice did she have though, Miss Parr called the shots and Sam dared defy her as she will end up in the dark room with the dolls.

The dolls

Sam's heart fluttered with the memory of just yesterday as they passed by the school gates. She hadn't stopped thinking about this but she wanted to. *How was it possible? Was it some kind of trickery?* Perhaps a cruel trick played by Miss Parr to just scare her into further submission.
They continued to walk up and now the back of the house was in sight to the right of them and through the trees she could see a green house at the back of the house she didn't even realise was there. She could see a large amount of plants lined up inside and thin white netted curtains that had slightly yellowed with age.
They had reached the gravelled, empty car park. A short brick wall surrounded it, and beyond that, steep embankments crowded with thick bush and foliage blocked the view.
At the heavy wooden double doors, Miss Parr produced the huge set of keys Sam had seen earlier. She flicked through them vigorously, the ring jangling in her hand, until she found a big, rusty brass key labeled "Front Door."
Miss Parr shoved the key into the lock and twisted hard. The mechanism grumbled before a low, reluctant click finally echoed out. She yanked the doors open, and together, they stepped back into the house.
The familiar, nauseating musty smell clogged Sam's senses. She trailed behind Miss Parr toward the door of the forbidden

wing. Without warning, Miss Parr snatched the bag from her hands — swift and greedy, like a gull tearing food from a tourist's fingers.

"Go and make me some Tea"

Miss Parr demanded and before Sam could even respond with a "Yes, Miss Parr" she had disappeared behind the mysterious door.

Upon turning to the opposite corridor she was confronted by a new horror. A sight that would be etched into her memory for the rest of her life. Her throat tightened as her peripheral vision was blurring, a cold chill creeped up her spine like a rolling wave of intense fear. The hairs again stood on end all over her body and for the first time began to question her sanity as she was staring into the eyes of a small child.

It was definitely a young boy of around five or six years old. It was hard to distinguish anything as from head to toe he was black and charred. Badly burnt with chunks of flaking red skin. Fused into his skin, he wore Victorian clothing. He had no eyelids either which exposed his bright blue but slightly bloodshot eyes. The child lifted his arm and pointed at Sam directly, his mouth slowly opened revealing just a blackness where his teeth and tongue should have been.

The child let out a low, rumbling roar—it sounded like a freight train barreling toward her. She couldn't scream. Couldn't move. The child's roar vibrated through her bones—then he vanished. Just like that.

Either Sam had lost her mind, or the house was truly haunted. Sam didn't like either of these options though. She had just seen a real ghost, the image of the burnt boy was still in her vision, like when you stare at something for so long and turn away and the image is still there in the form of light.

It took a few minutes for Sam to gather the strength to walk through the area where she just witnessed such a terror. She headed down the corridor and up the stairs to the Kitchen where she began to brew tea. It had only been a few days,shy of a week and Sam already felt like she was becoming an expert at making Tea.

Just finishing serving the tea and like clockwork Miss Parr had entered the room. As she sat down at the table, Sam walked over with the tea, careful not to spill it around the inside of the saucer it was on and placed it down on the table in front of her.

"Coaster"

Miss Parr hissed and Sam with quick reflexes pulled a coaster underneath the saucer.

Plucking up courage to do so, Sam began to pre think a question to her "Miss Parr, have you seen things around this house? Strange things?" Sam asked but Miss Parr just sipped on her tea with her pinky finger sticking out like a loose talon and had just ignored her question.

Sam knew that Miss Parr was hiding something, or actually not hiding it at all. She had made it obvious in that moment that it was a normal occurrence around the house or even still, orchestrated by her.

Artemis leapt onto the table and strolled towards Miss Parr, brushing himself against her and circling her tea. Sam was bewildered by the fact that a flea bag was allowed on the table, yet a coaster was needed for the tea.

"He wants his meal"

Miss Parr pointed at one of the bottom cupboards and Sam reached in to grab a box of Whiskas cat biscuits and poured a small amount into his bowl on the floor by the bin. Artemis leapt from the table with a small chirp as he landed on the kitchen floor and wasted no time in crunching down the biscuits with the side of his mouth and his head cocked to the side. Remus soon entered and darted for the remaining biscuits.

Miss Parr had briskly finished her tea and demanded the mug and saucer be washed and placed away neatly, with the other china. Artemis and Remus had long since finished eating and were now led in the windowsill, but eyes firmly on Sam, watching her every move.

Standing up from the table, Miss Parr waltzed out of the kitchen and headed back downstairs and left no further instruction or demands and then the faint sound of the mysterious door shutting.

Sam poured herself a glass of water from the tap and began to guzzle it down quickly, her eyes locked with both cats the whole time. She cleaned the glass and placed it back where she found it.

Sam, mentally exhausted since arriving on Tuesday afternoon, left the kitchen at six o'clock in the early evening. Artemis was still sitting in the window, watching the world go by.

Sam noticed the door, which had been locked previously, was

open. Sam couldn't resist the temptation to peek inside, the door slowly falling open with a creaking sound. It revealed a room full of glass bottles, they reminded her of the bottles she'd seen on the shelves in the shop earlier.

A large amount of the clear glass bottles were empty, but some of them had labels and had fluids inside them, so many different colours but a lot of green. One of the labels caught her eye with scribbled writing "Preserver" she hesitantly lifted the bottle and pulled out the deeply embedded cork top with a popping sound.

She brought the concoction to her nostrils and took a small inhale which instantly made her wretch, her eyes streamed as the smell was unlike anything she had ever had the misfortune to trial, she imagined that the smell was close to a rat crawling into a tight space, dying and then decomposing.

Sam quickly placed the cork back into the bottle and placed it back on the shelf.

She left the dimly lit room that reminded her of the book *George's Marvelous Medicine* and continued back up to the top of the house to her room. As she passed several windows within opened rooms she could see the sun was slowly beginning to set which caused a lump in her throat. Realising that she awaited whatever terror she would witness in the night to come.

16

FOUR MONTHS EARLIER

Violet sat on her bed in front of the smudged mirror as she brushed her long black hair. Long thin strands of hair danced away and floated across the room - occasionally capturing the glimmer of sunlight amongst the rays from the gap in the curtains. She adjusted the small silver locket necklace that hung from her neck.

She had been at the house for six weeks now, losing hope that she would ever be moved to a new home. Life had taken a darker turn in recent days. Miss Parr slashed at her face after being caught in the forbidden wing. This left a deep set of three scratches on her left cheek and it was now beginning to scab over, but now had erupted with green bruises.

Violet had already discovered part of the secret though, the driver, the office clerk at the orphanage and welfare officer were all in on this. Because they were all part of the same coven, they were modern day witches and not the good white magic-earth loving kind.

Continuing to run through the scenario in her head. The clerk, deeply embedded in the system, processed the documents, paperwork, and red tape needed to move the right child to Miss Parr's care. Then the welfare officer would sign it off without even checking it twice. The final step was the driver, while fairly insignificant, needed to be someone that wouldn't ask questions about the constant flow of children every six to eight weeks to the house.

But Violet didn't know what the endgame was yet, or what the motive was, she wanted to find out. The witch that ran the shop in town was also clearly in on it too. It was her slip up that led to Violet's shocking discovery. The old hag had left a book on the counter top that had documented everything, and included their weekly meetups too, which also included several other names that were not recognisable.

The night was drawing in now around the maze that was the house, and this also bought fear with it to Violet's thoughts. She had seen things since day one, stepping out of the car she witnessed seeing three other children at one of the windows. They were as clear as day to her, and she had questioned Miss Parr about them. This is when she also learned that something sinister awaited her fate there, as Miss Parr let out a small cackle.

Violet never believed in witches, vampires, ghosts, demons and the like. She read about them in books at the orphanage and this is how she quickly came to realise that Miss Parr was something peculiar.

She met all the classic cliche tropes that a witch had in the stories, even a similarity to the witch in *Snow White & The Seven Dwarfs* which was one of her favourite stories to read. She also reminded her of the witch from another story she read, it was an old one that she couldn't remember the name

of, but it featured a Lion in some fantasy world far away. Rain began to tap against the window now, small globular tears trickled down the glass and began to increase with quantity until eventually it was as if someone was throwing buckets of water against it. Then came the sound of the wind, it howled and cried through the wooden beams of the attic room like a shrieking spirit as it rattled the wardrobe doors. It caused the cherub faces etched on it to seem like they were blinking and moving their mouths in the shadows and then like a climactic ending to a story, a flash of bright white light lit up the room followed by a clap of roaring thunder.
Violet heard creaking coming from the other side of her bedroom door that alarmed her. At first there was a short stabbing creak, then a pause, and then a long chill inducing creak that rattled the entire room.
"Hello?"
No response came, and the air was sucked out of the room, along with the sound.
She could hear something.

Was it voices?

Violet crept over to the door slowly, occasionally stopping when the lightning lit up the room.
As violet reached the door, she realized it was trembling with the strength of the wind and rain, but the whispering continued. Violet placed her ear to the door slowly and reluctantly.

"Haaaaashhhhhhhhaaaaaahhhhhhhrrruuuuu"
Violet began to think it was the wind, it didn't sound like anything she could understand if it was a voice.

"GO TO BED"

The demonic voice burst through the door and flung its power around the room, bouncing off the walls like a tennis ball. Violet lost her breath and her footing and fell backwards onto the floor. Violet expected to see Miss Parr standing there, but the door was still shut.

She lay still for a moment, a million different things racing through her imagination. So many things had happened in the house, and yet every single time it occurred, it never seemed to stop being so terrifying.

Playing the voice back in her mind, it wasn't Miss Parr, it didn't sound human either. It sounded like it came from the darkest depths of a nightmare.

Get up, you are strong, you are not scared.

Even though Violet knew she was lying to herself, it was enough to encourage her to stand up and walk towards the door again. She had to know what or who was on the other side of the door, if anything at all.

Grabbing the door by the round and very cold brass handle, she turned it slowly, it seemed to turn forever before the door came slightly to. With a long groan the door opened, and just as she had expected, she was staring into nothing, just blackness of the staircase.

In this moment she had another wave of courage, she knew that Miss Parr would be fast asleep at this moment and it was her chance to unravel a mystery. She took this chance and began to descend down the stairs and into the dark void of the house.

She felt a slight excitement coursing through her veins, even though she was terrified.

Being a big reader she had essentially studied the Sherlock Holmes novels and now felt like she was right in the middle of one of those stories and expected Watson to come around the corner and give a false fright.

But upon reaching the corridor that seemed to never end, she realised she was totally and utterly alone.

Venturing further into the unknown, her footsteps seemed to push away clouds of settled dust on the long rug carpet that ran down the centre of the corridor. She passed a painting she always disliked, it was a woman, she was playing a violin with vines leading up her ankles.

Before long she found herself at the doorway of the kitchen and was now just above the doorway to the forbidden wing. This is where Violet began to have second thoughts about daring to go through with her investigation. Especially considering Miss Parr had already physically attacked her and drew blood.

Violet persistently walked down the last flight of steps and walked over to the door, this was it.

The handle on the door was larger and more modern. Although the entire wing ahead was a newer addition to the building it was purposefully built for whatever horror she was about to uncover.

She pulled down the handle and pulled the door open, it made no noise, it was so smooth compared to the rest of the doors in the house. Beyond the door was a small corridor, on the left was a double set of frosted glass doors. Another solid oak door sat to the right and then straight ahead was a sight that created a thick lump in her throat. Painted jet black and decorated with unrecognizable symbols, a locked door.

Slowly reaching for the handle, which was actually a small cherub's head. The sound of its turn made a childlike cry.

The door slowly fell open by itself with an inviting gesture to Violet. The room was filled with plantlife, bottles, endless books, and strange artifacts ranging from daggers, crystals, pendants, and bones. It stunk to high heaven of mold and decay. In the centre of the room sat a large round table with letters, numbers and words around the outside.

 A to Z of the alphabet, 0 to 9 numbered and then 'Yes' 'No' 'Hello' 'Goodbye'

In the centre of the table, there was a small wooden box with a latch on it. Carefully Violet flipped open the latch and carefully opened the box, aware that she also should avoid leaving fingerprints for the witch to find at first light. The contents of the box made her almost shriek in bile rising terror. There were teeth, nail clippings, locks of hair and an assortment of photos…. They were photos of children.

Violet's mind was blank at that moment, she didn't know how to react or what to do. She lost all train of thought, her emotions stripped of power, and her rational thought locked away. She hadn't even recognised that she was running to the front door of the house. She had no idea how much noise she had made in the heat of the moment. And because of this, Miss Parr was now awake and about to step out of her room. As reality slipped back into play like a cruel plot twist, Violet noticed the house had become deathly quiet once again and had become more aware of her senses. The front door was locked and the keys were most likely next to where the horrible woman slept. Violet began to wish she had never given into her curiosity, as she knew that curiosity killed the cat.

Turning back from the door, she crept back towards the staircase to retreat to her room, Violet had almost made it to the bottom step when she heard the croaking of floorboards behind her.

The familiar sense of dread swept over her, her breath became thin and goosebumps took over the skin of her arms. Then a wave of impending doom. Like all of the happiness had been sucked out of the world, leaving nothing but desperate hopelessness, And then finally the feeling of eyes watching, a predator fixated on its prey.

Any moment Violet felt like she would be yanked away into the darkness and never be seen again.

Summoning the courage to turn around, Violet was faced with the open doorway to the witches domain, it was now apparent that she was indeed awake now.

 Miss Parr's bedroom door was wide open and small flickering

candlelight illuminated the small entrance but it was quickly banished by a tall thin and imposing silhouette followed by Artemis at her side, sat watching and ready to spectate the imminent horror that awaited Violet as punishment.

"We don't like little children that snoop around in the night" Miss Parr's diction was perfect and clear, it was sharp and to the point and emitted a level of violent nature.

"I am s-"

"I AM SPEAKING NOW GIRL, I DIDN'T ASK FOR YOUR TONGUE TO BEGIN FLAPPING" she shrieked, the anger in her voice at fever pitch now and she became a snarling creature with every syllable that rolled from her as it echoed through the house.

"Now.. what to do with you" her voice now calmer but more sinister as Violet became too terrified to even look at her. Violet slowly began to sob which quickly erupted to full tears. Miss Parr's face became apologetic and sad herself, this sudden change had instantly confused Violet.

"Oh no.. did i make the girl cry?" Miss Parr was now shedding tears herself, it was a strange moment, but short lived as like a great actress she was able to flip the switch again and completely change, like a traffic light could go from red to green.

Miss Parr was now standing directly in front of Violet and towered over her, she seemed to have doubled in height and looked almost animatedly stretched in appearance. Her eyes turned pure black and hate filled, her grin turned sharp and beastly fangs on display as her hair blew in all directions even with no wind present.

The house fell dark and silent, no candlelight was present now and no spoken words, and even the lost and tortured souls of the stone foundations had retreated to sleep.

17

PRESENT DAY

Sam lay in bed, staring at the ceiling. Sleep wouldn't come. She had no idea what time it was. The events of the week replayed in her mind like a broken record.

She missed her friends at the orphanage, missed playing hide and seek in the endless hallways she used to think were a prison. But now, she understood what a real prison felt like. Sam had always been the oldest girl there. The younger ones looked up to her like a big sister. She'd tuck them in at night and tell wondrous stories about brave knights, fire-breathing dragons, and princesses chasing true love's kiss.

There had even been a boy at one point, Jamie Evans. He was her age, handsome in a scruffy sort of way. The boys were always a bit unkempt: untucked shirts, undone buttons, messy hair. Jamie reminded her of Peter Pan with his sharp jawline and mop of wild red hair. But unlike Peter Pan, Jamie was shy and rarely spoke to her.

Sam tossed and turned. She remembered the summer days spent racing barefoot through the garden, grass tickling her toes, the scent of blooming flowers in the air. She could still hear the echoes of laughter, blending with ringing phones, clacking keyboards, and the scratch of pens from the office staff.

She had been happy at the orphanage. The staff never

understood why she changed when placed in foster care. They never figured it out until it was too late. They'll listen this time, she thought, jaw clenched. It wasn't her. It was the system that was broken.

The more she considered it, the more it made sense. So many people came and went through the orphanage doors—it wouldn't be hard to slip through the cracks. Cheat the system. Disappear.

The room had gone still. In her daydreaming, something had shifted. She felt it first: a presence, watching her. But this time, the eyes didn't feel threatening. This was something new. A rhythmic thudding echoed around the bed. It came from all directions, walls, floor, ceiling—like a rubber ball bouncing unpredictably. And then, as if her thoughts had summoned it, a red rubber ball landed softly at the foot of her bed, the sound muffled by the sheets.

Sam froze.

Then, in one swift motion, she scurried across the bed in her grey t-shirt and striped knee-high socks, hoping Miss Parr wouldn't catch her dressed that way. She hated the moth-eaten nightgown Miss Parr had given her. She picked up the ball without hesitation. It was ice-cold.

She noticed her breath misting in the air. The temperature had dropped. Her skin prickled as she looked around the room, heart thudding. This felt like a grand entrance. Like the ghost from A Christmas Carol. *Expect the first ghost when the bell tolls one*, she thought, but the image of Gonzo and Rizzo from The Muppet Christmas Carol popped into her head. That had been a favorite back at the orphanage.

"Hello."

Sam nearly fell off the bed. a girl's voice.

Sitting where Sam had just been was a pretty girl, slightly younger than her. She had long black hair and wore the same dress Miss Parr had forced Sam to wear. A pendant necklace rested on her chest. Her skin was tinged grey-blue, the only real hint she was a ghost. She looked nothing like the charred Victorian boy Sam had seen before.
"Uh... hi," Sam said cautiously. Was this girl going to transform into something monstrous?
"I won't hurt you, Sam. It's okay." The girl smiled gently.
She knows my name.
"I just... are you..."
"Yeah, I know," the girl interrupted with a tired smirk, as if she'd answered the question a hundred times before.
"You need to escape this place and find help. She is dangerous."
She leaned forward. The smirk vanished, replaced with worry.
"Who is she?" Sam echoed, stunned. She knew Miss Parr was strange—unkind, even. But truly dangerous?
"I don't have much energy left," the girl said. "I wish I could

tell you everything, but I can't. She feeds off fear. This isn't like the fairytales. She can do terrible things."

The girl began to fade. Sam could see the bedframe and pillow through her.

"Don't waste time, Sam," the girl said. She reached out, but her hand vanished before it could touch Sam.

And then she was gone.

The room warmed. The ball still sat on the bed, etched into it were letters: V.I.O.L.E.T.

Pieces of the puzzle were falling into place. Sam wanted to run—wanted to escape. But a stronger part of her wanted to fight. She'd been running from her problems her whole life, always moved along, never given a say. Maybe this time she could change something. Not just for her. For the others, too. But what was Miss Parr doing? Did she kill children?

No. There had to be a reason. She told herself not to explore the house. If Miss Parr caught her, there'd be consequences. But curiosity itched at her. *No, no, no,* she repeated, clutching her head as if to fight off a splitting migraine.

Eventually, she calmed herself. She wouldn't go near the forbidden wing yet. But maybe the rest of the house held answers. Like the wine cellar, where she'd found the box labeled with Violet's name.   She crept into the corridor. Her plan: investigate the courtyard and the outbuilding past the fountain. The thick exterior walls would muffle any noise. You could barely hear the outside world from within the house unless it was storming.

As she padded quietly down the hall, she passed the painting of the violin woman. Something in her gut twisted. It was that strange, distant dread—like realizing too late you'd left the oven on. She took a few steadying breaths and turned to look.

The woman in the painting was gone.

Only the background remained: a wood-panelled wall, a grimy window, a moonlit sky.
Where is she?
The fear hit fast and deep, like discovering an infected wound, like a thousand paper cuts flaring all at once. A violent, scraping violin note slashed through the silence.
Out of the darkness emerged a figure—tall and impossibly thin, towering over her. It moved like a drunken puppet, jerking and twisting with unnatural speed, as if celebrating something awful.
The violin woman.
She played a sharp, manic tune, sawing at the strings with inhuman fury. Her face lacked features, only faint hollows where eyes and a mouth should have been. She didn't move like a person. She ran toward Sam, sprinting along the wall, the music speeding up with every second. Sam couldn't breathe. Couldn't move.
Then, with a burst of panic, she screamed.
The figure vanished as the violin clattered to the ground. The woman was gone—not in the painting, not anywhere. Sam

collapsed, drained. Her limbs shook. Her thoughts returned to Violet.

She feeds on your fear. Was this Miss Parr's doing? Was she summoning these horrors to keep Sam from discovering the truth? To drive her mad?

Sam forced herself upright, leaning against the wall. Every step back to her room was a struggle. If this was a tactic to keep her under control, how was she supposed to fight it? She didn't have the answer. Not yet.

But she thought about it for the rest of the long, cold night.

18

The next morning arrived with a ghoulish sight of grey clouds. Sam couldn't believe it had only been Monday gone that she arrived at the house. It was a very autumnal day from the view she had from her bedroom window. Distant trees had shed all signs of life as leaves of brown and yellow littered almost all of the car park. It wasn't raining but it was dreary outside and it seemed like it could start to spit at any moment.

A small money spider was climbing the window, its silky web was almost invisible as the little creature danced in what seemed like mid air. Sam didn't mind these small ones, she wouldn't go to handle them but she would happily sit and observe them. It spun its web as it glided across the width of the frame and disappeared into a small crack in the window frame. For a moment Sam was jealous of the spider, she imagined herself escaping through a crack herself and breaking free from the horrible nightmare she faced in the house.

Thoughts echoed back to her encounter with Violet's apparition the night before, and then to the violin woman she came face to face with in the dark corridor. She hadn't slept all night because of this and her eyes were dry and heavy as she stretched her arms out in the air forcefully as she took a moment to yawn.

Cleaning her glasses with her breath and bed sheets, Sam

stood and slipped on a pair of jeans and her t-shirt, she slipped on a pair of socks and then her slip-on brandless skate style shoes and opened her bedroom door. Before stepping out she closed her eyes, inhaled deeply through her nose and then exhaled from her mouth. She hesitated opening her eyes in case some demented creature or ghost was staring back at her. Luckily this wasn't the case right now.

Walking down the staircase, hands firmly sliding down the bannister. She had a funny thought to herself.

Why do ghosts come out at night? Why is it always the dead of night? She didn't show that she was laughing or chuckling to herself but she was in her mind. This question really hung onto her, like the money spider clinging onto its web.

She had now come to the corridor where the violin woman was, stopping at her painting. She was there, it was back to its hideous normal and haunting self but she still felt eyes on her as she continued to walk past it, Sam found herself quickly skipping in her step to increase her distance from it as fast as possible.

The house was still, the rooms were closed and this included the room with the dolls inside, she shuddered as she walked past it, she couldn't avoid going by it if she wanted to get anywhere else in the house.

Reaching the kitchen to her surprise Miss Parr wasn't there waiting on her tea. The cat's food bowl was half empty and the food was fairly fresh, she couldn't have long been here.

The mist shrouded the church steeple from the view of the window.

Pouring herself a glass of water, tempted by the apple juice sitting in the fridge. Knowing she wouldn't dare to touch it without permission. She took a few gulps of the water and then emptied out the remaining slither at the bottom of the glass, rinsed and polished the glass and placed it back carefully. Taking the end slice of bread from its packet, she knew that Miss Parr hated the end pieces so it would be OK. She placed it in the toaster and pulled down the mechanism. Waiting beside the toaster, the room was a horrible off white colour. It clearly hadn't ever been repainted. Her thoughts were interrupted by the toaster's ejection of the lightly toasted bread. She carefully spread butter over it and made sure to clean up any crumbs, and wash the knife carefully.

Sitting at the table, Sam enjoyed every bite of her slice of toast. Wishing she could have used some Jam from the fridge but if she wasn't going to have some of the juice, she certainly wouldn't dare to take any of the expensive locally made Jam. She examined the calendar pinned to the wall with each bite. It was two years old, and no days had been crossed out.

The chair she was sitting on was very uncomfortable, it had no cushion and so she was sitting on cold and solid wood. Slim spindles framed the backrest like ribs in a cage, and the thick, flat arms protruded out awkwardly, as though once meant to comfort but now only to restrain. The seat, broad and grooved with the patterns of age, bore the polished sheen of decades' worth of use—too smooth, almost slippery, as if someone had sat there far too long. Below, its turned legs stood sturdy and defiant, one slightly askew, giving the impression it might

creak or tip with the wrong kind of touch.
The table didn't match the chairs around it, in fact one of the chairs was completely different, darker in colour and had a royal red cushioned base.
Before long, the toast was just crumbs on a plate, Sam gave another stretch and a yawn and pushed the seat with the back of her legs, it made a long whining low rumble across the floor which seemed to disturb parts of the house with a ghostly echo.
Walking back over to the sink with her plate and washing it thoroughly, Sam was feeling even more tired and slightly giddy now she had eaten. She placed the plate back with its family and headed out of the kitchen door.
She could hear the faint ticking of a clock that was sitting in the reception area just at the bottom of the staircase to her left. Remus interrupted his meal, waiting for her to leave the kitchen before he returned.
Thinking about the courtyard again, Sam excitedly ran down the flight of stairs and into the reception area, she would have to go through a set of glass doors that she hadn't been through to get there.
Going through these doors, her face caught a soft touch from a spider's web and she recoiled in fear, she immediately rubbed her face with her hands in a blind panic and was terrified that a large spider had now landed on her. There was no sign of one and she sighed with relief.
Connecting the reception room to the next room. She faced a glass corridor. Which was behind another set of frosted double

doors. There wasn't much to see outside of the corridor, it was just empty space between two exterior brick walls, there was some drainage in the concrete floor, and weeds escaping the gaps in the concrete, clearly looking for an escape route wherever it can grow next.

The corridor was significantly colder than the main part of the house, she could imagine in the summer it would be unbearable stuffy in there though.

Entering the double doors, it was a smaller square room that Sam believed to be leading to the courtyard. This room had a winding staircase that went up, she could see all the way to the roof and it reminded her of a lighthouse. The staircase was broken off at the top and its steps were old and unstable, it didn't look safe to use.

The doors to the courtyard were very heavy to push open, Sam's feet slipped backwards as she pushed them open and now she regretted not wearing a jumper or coat because she was outside and it was cold to the point in which she felt it in her bones, it was a very fresh feeling cold though, the air in her nostrils felt good and it did wake her up further like a natural coffee effect.

Sam realised her hands were black with dirt from the doors she just pushed open, she brushed her hands together with disgust but it didn't help at all, it was just causing a smudged look, she nearly brushed it on her jeans before sharply coming to her senses that she didn't want to ruin them or show that she'd been exploring the house.

The courtyard was bigger than she remembered from the

window before, it stretched out in an almost hexagon shape and in the centre sat the fountain with a goblin-like creature at the top but there was no water present at all, it was bone dry and had clearly been for some time and moss had begun to grow all over the fountains two tiered bowls.

The exterior of the walls towered over the courtyard as she felt eyes from all the windows around her, she thought that Miss Parr could be standing at any of them, but so could the many spirits that she had come to encounter in the house, it felt like the house was alive itself.

Pigeons flapped playfully around on the surrounding rooftops, trees swayed in the distance to the slow calming winds, it was very quiet and was almost eerie, like standing in someone's grave. Thinking about the potential children buried all over the courtyard, thinking she would end up with them soon, tears fell from her cheeks as she was feeling vulnerable, possibly more so now because she was standing amongst endless windows, endless possibilities for something to be watching her.

Sam was feeling sorry for herself as she perched herself onto an old mossy and slightly broken wooden bench on the side of the courtyard. She didn't know why she deserved so many bad experiences.

Is it me?

She thought to herself as she wiped away tears from her eyes that had now increased in size and frequency, small pearl-like tears continued to fall onto the jagged concrete beside her feet as she leaned forward and placed her hands over her face.

Numbness overcame her like an unavoidable tidal wave. She was being pulled by emotions that she didn't understand. *Was she feeling sad, guilty, pain, self pity? What were any of these feelings?*
Snapping out of it as quickly as the feelings had emerged. She stood up with determination, and moved towards the out house on the other side of the courtyard.
It was too dark to see anything but she could tell there was a large open space, it reminded her of a church with the pews all in a perfect line, but there were no visible signs of a religion. Walking around the exterior, she tried to slide open a window with a push. She peered inside the locked window. It was useless, all she could see was darkness, and her own reflection.
Defeated, Sam turned around to head back to the house. She walked through the courtyard and back into the connecting glass corridor.
Upon going into the double doors of the reception area, she noticed it was still eerily quiet, you would be able to hear a pin drop, it was so quiet that Sam could hear the blood rushing to head through her ears.
The front door burst open and Miss Parr waltzed through, Sam's reality came crashing down as she was enjoying the time she was not present.
"What are you doing?"
Miss Parr took off her coat, she was wearing a long black dress and it looked as though she'd been to a party.
Sam went in with a compliment, hoping it would build a better

relationship between them.

"You look really nice in that dress today Miss Parr"

Sam smiled, but Miss Parr saw right through it.

"If i wanted your opinion i'd ask for it, who are you to give your thoughts on what i look like"

Miss Parr hung up her coat and stormed off into her wing, slamming the door closed behind her and out of sight.

Sam was about to walk away but Miss Parr quickly appeared again a few moments later, this time with a cardigan over the top of her dress.

"I am going to have guests tonight, you will not leave your room you understand? I don't want to see or hear you"

Miss Parr stood with her arms crossed and continued

"You'll dine an hour earlier and vanish"

she hissed as she stormed off again.

Sam wondered who the guests could be and then curiosity got the better of her as she quickly poked her hands in the coat that Miss Parr had just hung up, but they were empty.

19

As day turned to darkness and the clock struck seven, Sam sat in the library reading *Frankenstein* by Mary Shelley. She struggled with the old-fashioned language and unfamiliar words.
Guests had been arriving at the house in the cover of night, Sam couldn't get an angle to catch a glimpse of them. She could hear the cars pulling up in the loud gravel car park. Placing the book back on the shelf once she had read at least twenty pages, She couldn't concentrate—none of the characters felt real to her.
Her mind drifted to the out house that she tried to explore. Imagining what it was used for. Sam thought maybe the guests would gather there, after all the rest of the house was too small to house the amount of people coming into the house that she could hear, a short while ago when she had just started reading she could hear a lot of commotion, so there must have been quite a few people there at the house.
Her best vantage point would be the corridor with windows that overlooked the courtyard. It was risky considering it was so close to the black door that was secretive. If it was the out house that was for the guests, she would get a clear view of it from there.
Sam pulled over a striped and baggy black and grey jumper and hurried out of her bedroom once again. She had really

begun to find her way around the house now on her little exploration missions.

Passing by the violin woman painting again, Relieved to see she was still there, not in the corridor waiting with her dreadful music. As she moved further into the house she could hear the chinking of glasses and cutlery, some laughter and the occasional door closing.

Sam went down another flight of steps and turned several corners through endless corridors, no matter how much she walked down them it was still quite confusing to find her way but she was getting better at it now.

She came to the corridor with the windows and got onto her hands and knees, slowly crawling over to the window and peering around it, careful not to be spotted.

The outhouse was the center of the party.

She could see a lot of movement inside passing by candlelight. The flickering flames danced around in the darkness.

There was a creaking sound to her right, turning her head she realised the black door was swinging open on its own. It was creepy, Sam didn't like the way she was feeling, the temperature dropped quickly as she could see her breath again. She knew at this moment that meant something else was with her.

Trusting her gut instinct, she crawled past the windows and stood up, she cautiously walked towards the doorway, all she could see was a turning to the right but ahead was a red painted wall and several skulls and bones as trophies. She stopped to look at them and try to identify them, there were definitely deer antlers, but there were unidentifiable bones too. Taking the right turn, she was now in a small room that had endless amounts of taxidermy on display, from birds and owls to cats, dogs and rats.it had a horrific and peculiar smell, it was a musty smell that could only belong to something that had crawled into a corner some time ago and died. Sam had smelt it before, in the orphanage a boy called Oliver, a strange boy that always carried a large backpack around with him, one day he pulled out a dead squirrel that was decomposing, everyone around him screamed in terror as the staff rushed to take it away from him. Another time he was caught taking fish out of the tank in the reception, and letting them flop around in the bottom of his bag.

A cold chill clawed up Sam's spine, she shuddered uncontrollably as if someone had walked over her grave or even danced over it. Her vision doubled as she felt an overwhelming sense of dread. The panic was justified by the flapping of wings, a meow, a bark, a squeak, and the noises of a dozen different animals. The taxidermy came alive, a deer's head on a plaque was screaming in pain. The deafening roar of the animals was unbearable and made the floorboards tremble, Sam was struggling to keep balance as she tried her hardest to quickly escape the room.

The black door in front of her slammed shut and the sound of the lock clicked, she bashed at the door with her fists and screamed louder than she'd ever screamed before, the sounds of the animals still blaring and now a crow had swooped down at her, pecking at her head and pulling at her hair. She swiped over and over again as she spun in circles on the spot trying to rid of the bird. Feathers fall around her in slow motion as she feels hot sticky liquid flow down the side of her face over her cheek, it was her blood and the crow was not showing any signs of stopping its relentless pecking. Its eyes were lifeless when it made eye contact with Sam, it had nails through its feet from being on display.

Sam stopped and gathered all her might, she swiped with her arm and knocked the bird to the ground, now it was not moving, still in the pose it was in when on display. With that the animal noises came to a halt, and there was absolute deafening silence once more.

. The door clicked, like an unseen force was now allowing her to leave the room, she didn't waste any time in leaving, opening the door, looking back into the still room, to see just feathers floating through the air, she left and closed the door behind her.

Crouching at the window and taking a second to feel the wound on her scalp with her fingers. It was a fairly deep gash that had spilled blood down one side of her face. Using her jumpers sleeve to wipe her eyes of blood, it had unfortunately mostly dried up already and left blotches on her face.

The door to the out house swung open, and out stepped a familiar face. It was the driver, Sam found this odd because he was just a contractor for the orphanage, *wasn't he?*

20

The pointy chinned man, with the swept back black hair placed a cigar into his mouth and bit the end, he spat it out on the floor and flicked open a lighter with chubby fingers. puffing on it until smoke began to rise. He exhaled dark grey smoke with his eyes closed and a soft relaxed smile.
He wiped off any fragments of ash from his tuxedo carefully with the tips of his fingers and straightened his jacket.
"Mr Penny" nodded another lady who had just stepped outside from the same doorway, she wore a thin black dress, quite short as it hung around her thighs. She had a large black hat with a bow on it, similar to something a mother would wear at a wedding and she was smoking a cigarette on one of those sticks you only saw rich people use in the movies.
"Charming night 'mam" smiled Penny, his voice was rough like sandpaper, as if he had smoked 100 cigars that very night.
"Will you be partaking in tonight's extra activities?" the woman smiled with a secretive expression. Her heavy make-up hides any wrinkles, it would be difficult to assume her age.
"Of course, I wouldn't miss it, not on the eve of Moloch" he smiled as he stubbed out his cigar on the wall. He gave a nod to the woman and headed indoors out of sight, the woman followed.

Sam led back against the wall, her hands were shaking, she was facing the window with her legs spread outward. Exhausted after yet another grizzly encounter in the house and now plucking up the strength to move back towards her bedroom.
Crawling on her hands and knees once again, she used her remaining energy to sneak back past the large windows and took to the staircase where she dragged herself to her feet.
The temptation to fall down and sleep was strong. Each time she experienced something in the house it seemed to take something from her, all energy and strength was zapped away in seconds and it seemed to get worse with each event.
With this tiredness, there was a realisation that she had lost all bearings of where she was in the house.
Sam screamed and dived for one of the many side doors. She slammed it shut behind her. The music stopped. So did the laughter.

Silence.

It wasn't comforting—just a different kind of threat. But anything was better than that.
A sudden image flashed through her mind, a memory.
She was at a funfair. Standing on wet, muddy ground in her welly boots. She was smaller. Younger. Her mouth wouldn't work—no words would come. The smell of popcorn, candy

floss, and hot dogs wafted through the air.

Screams and laughter surrounded her, voices blending into a dizzying cacophony. Dodgems crashed, merry-go-rounds spun, lights flashed. Every direction was movement. Blurred, faceless figures rushing past on rides.

She felt it then. Fear. Lost in the crowd. No one is familiar in sight.

Her balloon slipped from her tiny fingers. She watched it rise and float away. Without thinking, she followed it, arms outstretched, toddler hands grasping at the air.

The balloon drifted into a small striped tent. Drawn to it, as if pulled by an invisible thread, she followed.

Inside, a makeup table glowed under a ring of bulbs. Scattered across the surface were pots of face paint and lipstick. A foam head with a red clown nose sat silently on display.

A man sat at the table with his back to her, powdering an already white-painted face.

He caught her gaze in the mirror, smiled, then spun around.

He towered above her now, twice her size and growing. She sank into the muddy floor, shrinking, helpless.

"Come sit on my lap and I'll tell you a story," he whispered, reaching out with gloved hands.

Darkness swallowed her.

Sam jolted awake. In total darkness, she sat slumped against the door. A faint reflection glimmered in front of her—distorted, like a funhouse mirror.

Yeah great that's all I need now, my reflection.
She turned to the left. There it was—stretched into an impossibly thin version of herself. To the right, another, this time absurdly wide, her face three feet across.
She stood shakily, heart still hammering.
A mirror maze.
She placed her hands out in front, palms brushing the cold, damp surface of glass. It felt gritty in places, dusty, dirty. She wiped her hands together and continued forward, carefully tracing her way.
Every direction was the same. Walls of glass, some sharp with reflection, others dimmed or warped. She turned left, then right. Took a cautious step, and hit a wall. Pain bloomed on her forehead. Her head was already sore.
She turned around, then tried again. Another left, then a dead end. She backtracked. Every so often, a light flickered in the distance, reflected from somewhere—but from what, she couldn't tell.
It felt like the maze was shifting, mirrors rearranging behind her.
She stopped, fighting to breathe. The pressure in her chest was rising. *Not now. Not a panic attack. Not here.*
She stared into the nearest mirror. Her reflection looked pale, wild-eyed.
You can do this. This isn't real. This place is screwing with your head, Sam.
She inhaled deeply, puffed out her chest. Rolled her shoulders. Clicked her neck.

Then pressed on.
Left. Another left. A sharp right.

She halted.

Her reflection stood before her again—but this time, it wasn't mimicking her movements. It just smiled.
Unease crawled through her body like icy fingertips going up her spine.
No. Not stopping. Not giving in.
She moved past it, brushing the cold glass as she pressed forward. The maze continued, endless and strange. At one point, she jumped—hoping to see over the walls—but they reached higher than she thought.
She was trapped.
 She felt the touch of a small hand as it pulled her through the path quickly, left, right, left, left, left, right and then she had lost sense of direction. The figure was still in darkness in front of her but it was clearly a small child.
They came to a door which flew open in front of them, a bright white light that was impossible to look at poured into the room and flooded Sam's vision. The touch of the hand had vanished and without warning, Sam was back in her room, standing looking at the wardrobe she hated, its cherub faces haunting her mind once more.
What the fuck just happened?
Sam rarely swore, but she thought it was safe to think it. Thinking back to the conversation with Violet's apparition

earlier, trying to make sense of what she just witnessed. A feeling of hopeless insanity swooped over her and took control, she found herself grasping her hair and tugging at it, screaming to herself on her knees.

I am losing my mind, I can't control myself. I am losing my mind. I can't control myself. I am losing my mind. I can't control myself.

This endless loop filled every thought, every corner of her mind subjected to this absolute uncontrollable aggression, confusion, sadness, depression. She began to sweat, her ears ringing, her skin tingling, she felt woozy and unsteady, her eyes shook from left to right uncontrollably and her mouth became bone dry in seconds and she forced a cough to feel like she could breathe again.
Collapsing in a heap of her own sweat and mindless confusion, she quickly passed out, her vision fading to black and out of focus, like her brain just collapsed under the weight of her own sanity, as she drifted off into a peaceful sleep she heard a whisper.
"Sleep, rest. You need your strength"

21

It still looked inherently evil. The stone, chipped away in places, whispered ghost stories, while the windows gave the house a cruel, watchful expression.

Eyes opened amongst the dust that several hours prior, had been disturbed. She coughed as she inhaled some as she awoke. She was lying on the floor and remembered that she passed out. Her throat was dry and as sharp as razor blades, with each attempt at swallowing the only saliva she had remaining, which tasted gritty and dusty.

Pushing herself up onto her knees with the palm of her hands, immediately wiping off the dust and grit on them. She brushed down her clothes but she felt disgustingly unclean.

Placing an ear to the door, she listened for the sounds of the remaining guests, it was silent but the house was too big to consider this evidence of them leaving.

Grabbing a change of clothes, her last clean set. She stepped out of her bedroom and paced down the stairs with the intention to have a bath. Excited about the prospect of feeling like a human being again following what felt like she had rolled in the mud.

Sam slipped into one of the bedrooms that had an ensuite, and turned the cold steel taps, each half way giving an even blend of hot and cold water that was now trickling into the bathtub. Pausing again, she stood by the door of the room, her ears tuning into any noises that might indicate that people were still in the house.

Waiting for the tub to fill to acceptable depth, she sat on the edge of the bed, tempted to lie down and rest her eyes, but she knew that would be a mistake and she would most likely fall asleep. Imagining herself waking up to an overflowing bath, a flooded corridor and Miss Parr with a monstrous torture device being prepared for her. an Iron Maiden (one of those coffins with hundreds of nails in them)

Her mind was skimming events of the previous night. The clown and the funfair burnt into her mind. It felt like a secret that had been behind a locked door for many years and that now, this house had given her the keys.

Diving into her newly discovered and unlocked memories distracted Sam, and she quickly hurried back to the running water and turned the taps in the opposite direction to interrupt the flow of water. Placing one leg in to test the temperature and then the other leg followed, and she quickly descended onto her back and closed her eyes.

The tap was dripping with a slow rhythm that was calming to her, she tapped her toe on the porcelain tub to the beat of the drip. Attempting to clear her mind of everything and focus on the warmth of the water that surrounded her, and the peaceful silence.

After some time as the water became much cooler, she decided it was time to get out, she dried herself quickly and changed into her black joggers and plain white tee.

Yanking on the plug of the bath to drain the water, she then glanced over at the mirror and observed herself, she began to stare deep into her own eyes and tried to think rationally about what had occurred in the house all week.

Outside of the door she heard the creaking of floorboards and shuffling, she stayed still as she tried to listen to the noise to confirm what it was.. Nothing, silence.

Inhaling a breath, she held it and opened the door quickly. Thinking the clown would be facing her. The violin woman, or the burnt child. But it was neither of them.

"Hello?"

There was no answer, she expected to hear a ghostly disembodied voice and her imagination ran wild with possible responses. Luckily nothing happened, which also just made things more eerie.

Walking back up to her bedroom, finally reaching the staircase that led directly to the door she heard the noise again behind her, a shuffle or a dragging sound.

"Miss Parr?"

Again there was no answer.

Feeling like a headache was coming, Sam massaged her temples with her index fingers and closed her eyes. She stood halfway up the stairs and felt herself lean with slight dizziness. Perhaps it was the tiredness making her feel this way, but she felt unwell quite suddenly.

Once spending six months in hospital, she was no stranger to illness. She had suffered with Covid-19 quite badly during that pandemic. That kind of illness would spread like a plague through an orphanage and there was only one or two out of nearly 50 children who managed to avoid it.

She had not quite been the same since. Her immune system was compromised as she was often getting colds.

Opening the door and stumbling through, she clutched her head with the palm of her hand, she felt hot to the touch and was burning up quite significantly.

Arched over she hit the bed considerably hard, the bed bounced her up and down violently due to the old springs, sounding like a trampoline.

Groaning to find a comfortable position she held the crook of her arm over her eyes and slowly fell asleep.

She awoke to complete darkness, but there was faint singing, it was like a distant choir. It immediately made Sam feel uncomfortable. It was two in the morning, who on earth could be singing at two in the morning?

Still fully dressed, her thin and trembling frame rose from the bed slowly and she made her way back out of her room. Her head was significantly better, but there was still a dull ache. Made worse if she moved her head excessively.

With tiptoes down the stairs, she slowly made her way down, trying to follow the sound of the singing that was still ringing through the house, it seemed to be bouncing off of everything from the walls, the windows, the doors and all the furniture. In quicker succession she walked past the violin woman's painting, again checking that she was still there, in which she was thankfully in Sam's mind. The last thing she wanted was another encounter with that thing right now.

Through double doors and down the next staircase, she passed through all the spare rooms, and down another flight of stairs towards the Kitchen. Glancing at the door which held the dolls, she couldn't think about those right now either.

The singing was much louder, it seemed to be coming from outside. It was a low droning chant now, and an organ played. It was much like a church gospel, but something seemed off, perhaps the key.

She could see lit candles, hundreds of them in the reception room below. They covered every possible surface area.

Before heading down the final staircase, she thought about Miss Parr and her instructions that she was not to show her face to the guests. But she had to know what was going on. After some hesitation, her foot touched the top step, and then the next. It slowly became easier to walk down with confidence, the sound was coming from the courtyard. The out house was still being occupied by the guests.

As she opened the double doors into the glass corridor she passed through earlier, she noticed a small glowing pair of eyes at the end in front of the doors to the courtyard. It was Artemis, the nightmare guardian himself.

He let out a deep stomach originating groan as soon as Sam came into view. He puffed his tail as he raised his back legs.

"Get out of my way"
Sam hissed back this time.
Artemis stepped forward with a careful step, looking like he was now going to pounce as his chin pressed against the floor and another groan came from deep within him, almost like there was a demon possessing him.
Sam slowly took off one of her trainers and held it up for protection, knowing that the cat could pounce at her.
"You don't scare me"
This time Artemis let out a violent hiss, like a warning, that it was not too late to walk away. Sam continued to now step forward, and tried to walk around the cat.
The feline eyes locked on her.
Artemis pounced through the air and scratched her forearm, then again from behind in the same place, and again at her ankle, Artemis' teeth sunk into her with a screeching hiss.
Sam kicked her leg and the cat flew back to the floor, landing on all fours and looking ready to pounce again.
"Get away!"
Clutching her arm that was now bleeding from a deep scratch, her ankle was OK, but clearly had some broken skin on the surface. Quickly opening the doors to the courtyard, as she slammed them closed she could see Artemis running towards her before they closed shut.
Evil thing, dreadful thing, what the hell is wrong with it.
The singing from the out house had become obvious again, she realised it had almost been the perfect soundtrack to Artemis' lunging at her, like something out of a horror movie.

There was a red glow in all of the windows of the out house with large human shadows cast against the walls inside, the lyrics of the song were not recognisable other than several lines that repeated "He is with us, He'll be with us in blood." There was a strong smell that danced through the courtyard in a mist, it was a combination of Lavender, Lemon but then some other smells that were unrecognisable but very strong. Sam was crouched as she moved quickly towards the window. Inside the outhouse, Candle Lights flickered. Miss Parr stood in a long black robe, towering over the others that were sitting down. It was similar to a church layout. Lit up like a half moon, faces sat in partial darkness. Miss Parr was lit by candles around her.
"My friends, thank you once again for a glorious celebration of Moloch"
Raising her hands in the air, a large statue sat behind, an owl. Its eyes lit by candles. The wings wrapped around the side of the raised floor where she stood.
"It was forty years ago when you saved me. I was weak, a foolish girl that believed in fairytales. Tales that I would be able to live a life of pleasing others. Give to others and receive nothing in return. I had no strength, or voice of my own"
She was shouting out, looking deadpan to the back of the room, not making eye contact with anyone that was sitting down and watching her.
"I promised you, that the children of this town would provide us with new life. A restoration of our old, decaying vessels and it has put us closer to him."

Her hands curled into claw like shapes that bounced a flickering shadow of a monster on the back wall.

"Closer to him" the crowd chanted.

Sam tried to swallow the lump that was in her throat, but it wouldn't budge, her hairs were again standing on end and a cold sweat had begun to seep through her pores.

Shadows of movement cast up on the high interior roof of the out house, it was like demons dancing across the old beams of wood that crossed over each other and a small wooden chandelier was dangling left and right.

The driver was now walking towards Miss Parr through the aisle, he was carrying something in his arms.

It was a child, much to Sam's horror. He had blonde hair that was neatly brushed to one side. There was no movement, his eyes closed and his body was totally lifeless as the driver placed him down on a stone altar, in front of Miss Parr.

"Young life gives us strength, it gives us purpose, it allows us to do his work" Miss Parr raised her left hand clutching a dagger, it was hard to make out in the darkness with just a slight reflection of the candlelight but it was a ceremonial dagger for certain- With a quick swipe she cut the boys throat and blood trickled down into a chalice held by the Driver, who after a few moments, handed it back to Miss Parr and scurried back to his seat.

Sam watched in horror, she couldn't move as she was watching the blood dripping down off the boy's neck and dripping off the altar.

"With this blood, we will be born again"

"Born Again"

Miss Parr pulled out a vial that looked like the same liquid Sam saw in the bottle room before. Scribbled on its label, the word Preserver.

She poured the contents into the Chalice and lifted it above her head, in doing so the audience lifted to their feet and the organ began to play.

The singing that erupted was deafening. She could hear the bass of the music vibrating the glass and the wooden window frame Sam was grasping. Miss Parr sipped from the Chalice, and moved to the front row as each person also sipped.

Sam felt sick to her stomach, she felt as though every drop of hope she ever had was gone, swallowed by evil.

Survival instincts now took hold, Sam rushed to her feet and slammed through the double doors, she hopped over Artemis who she had caught unaware as he was cleaning himself. Continuing to push through the next set of doors and through the reception room, she wasted no time and kicked open the front doors.

Gravel shifted under running feet as she sped through the car park and onto the pavement aside the main road, she had no idea where the police station was but she was going there.

She ran down the pathway towards the school, still hearing the singing and the slight glow from the outhouse as she passed the treeline that backed onto it, she saw a blurred glimpse of faces through the trees lit by a blood red candlelight as she ran.

She didn't look back now, running past the locked school

gates and past the horse field, the horses were not there at that moment, probably wanted to flee just as she was from the nearby evil intent.

She passed houses that had lit pumpkins in the windows and on the steps outside the front doors, but it was eerily quiet for halloween night. There were no trick or treaters, no one walking around, no sound other than a distant dog barking.

She continued to run down the steep turning path. Heading towards the top of the big steep hill leading into town.

Police station, where is it?

She had slowed now, feeling slightly safer that she was a good distance from the house now.

Still no sign of life, she was now walking slower as she was trying to catch her breath, she was weary of walking down the hill past all the darkened alleyways and through the foul litter covered pavement.

Moments passed, and she had reached the high street. It was dark and there was no one around. No sounds, no cars or anything but the occasional buzzing street lamp. They were Victorian lamps that had been modernised to be electric. Each of them seemed to be a different shade of white or yellow, one of which flickered constantly.

There was an old victorian brick archway across the street, it had old paintings of victorian faces on them, but Sam's heart fluttered as she saw a dark figure move in the distance between them.

Swiftly moving on, walking down the street passed all the blacked out closed shops, she passed the shop she visited earlier and wondered if the creepy old woman was at the house with the others.

She came across a pub that had lights on, its sign 'The Angel' was swinging when there seemed to be little breeze. She could see lanterns dimly lit inside the old criss-crossed windows. With the push of the door, her senses greeted. A warmth from the fireplace, the smell of beer, the smell of old leather and a hint of unclean toilets.

"You ok there love?"

A large ginger haired woman from behind the bar was looking at Sam while she was pouring a pint. The pub was quiet with only a few men dotted around the seating. One of them wore a flat top hat, his fist holding up his chin and he was looking blankly into the fireplace. Another, looked like an old sailor, in all the fishing gear, it was cliche as had a big white bushy beard and a black sailors hat and puffed on a pipe as stared at Sam. There was another man at the bar, and a couple of men talking in the corner of the room.

"I said, are you OK love?"

The woman reinforced now with some concern on her face.

"I need help, where is the police station?"

Sam was shaking uncontrollably, both from fear and from the cold night she had just taken refuge from.

"Well it's back up the marlborough road, halfway up the hill love! - Come, take a seat"

She took the nearest seat to the door without any hesitation. The stool made a terrible dragging sound across the cold, tiled stone floor.

"Hot Chocolate?"

The ginger barlady was mopping up spilt beer across the bar with a guinness tea towel.

"I haven't got any money, sorry."

"Don't be daft, ere, its on the house"

She smiled as she turned to the big machine behind her, and pressed one button that ejected a small cup. It whizzled and frothed and seemed to be finished in an instant.

Sam choked in terror, suddenly she realised all the eyes of the men were now looking at her with mysterious intent, the old sailor stood up and started laughing with his hands on his oversized beer belly and his yellow rotting teeth exposed.

A weasel of a man was staring at her from the corner of the room. He had long brown matted hair on either side of his head and a large bald patch in the middle, looking like a mad scientist from a comic book.

Sam couldn't help but make eye contact, he cocked his head.

"Ere, haven't i seen you some place"

Sam just smiled and looked at the floor, the ginger lady placed the hot chocolate on the table, smiled and wandered off to the bar again. The man still looking at Sam, he licked his lips, like a cartoon cat, that had spotted a cooked meal.

"You're the girl that Florence looks after arn't yer?"

Sam panicked and jumped off the stool. She backed out of the door, not turning away from them and she bumped into another man walking in, who just stared at her.

Sam began to run up the high street again, hearing laughter behind her

22

Sam turned onto Marlborough Road, she was sweating and out of breath as she had run some fair distance. She wiped her forehead with her forearm and held her knees to recuperate. The road was full of houses on either side but was a steep incline all the way back up to the other side of the Graveyard and would eventually meet the house again in a big loop. There were cars parked all the way up the road on either side, packed in tightly together and there was a small woodland area that separated the pavement and the houses on one side. She came up to a primary school, where there was a zebra crossing and a sign that said police station, Finally.
The police station was just like the other houses, Victorian brickwork, white painted and sometimes rotted wood frames around the windows and a big bay window, in fact you wouldn't recognise it as a police station at all.
About to open the door and walk in, the door opened itself and on the other side stood a policeman, wearing a classic vest with a walkie talkie on his chest. He was a middle aged man with a thick but well shaped mustache and piercing brown eyes and slicked back hair. "Are you OK?"
The man looked at Sam, concerned at her current state, which was covered head to toe in sweat and out of breath.
"I need help, I've seen Miss Parr up at the mansion kill a young boy" Sam was crying now, she couldn't hold back the

emotion any longer.

Strangely the policeman didn't have much of a reaction at all. "Come through, let's talk" he ushered Sam through the door and guided her through the corridor to a small interview room. It was nothing like the movies or the tv shows. There was no big mirror where people sat watching. It was a room with a door, no windows and just a table and chairs. A recording device in the middle of the table.

The policeman placed a small plastic cup of water from the cooler in front of her with the other arm touching her shoulder. "Drink this"

She gulped it down fast, still shaking.

"So you're the girl that Miss Parr has taken in huh?" he asked. Sam just nodded.

"My name is Richard, you are safe with me OK Sam?"

She paused for a brief moment, and expressed a puzzled look. "How do you know my name?"

"Well - you just told me!" he smiled, but it was unconvincing and menacing.

He continued, "Everyone knows everybody around here, don't worry about it."

Sam felt slightly unnerved.

"OK, tell me what's going on," Richard asked as he pulled out a small notebook and pushed the button on his pen.

Leaving out the creepy moments. Sam told him the story from her arrival.

Still Richard showed no reaction to her story, no facial expression at all as he wrote it down.

"Listen Sam, i am not sure what it is you think you saw, Miss Parr is a staple of the community and we've never really had any problems with her up there"
"I know what I saw, and it wasn't just her, there is an entire party of people up there"
She was crying again.
Richard smiled, this upset her even more.
"I'm just going to make a call, I'll be right back"
Richard got up and put his notepad and pen back into his vest pocket and walked out of the room, the door locked with a click.
She bashed on the door with her fists clenched.
Screaming with her face pressed against the door.
There was no response, Sam furiously kicked over the chair she was sitting on and slid her back down against the corner of the room and hugged her legs, getting as small as she could.
Imagination was running wild in her mind.
What would she do to me?
And then her thoughts were to the other people who blindly followed her in the audience like members of a brainwashed cult.
Was Richard there? Is he one of them?
This thought was terrifying, having the police in her pocket would mean there was no escape.
A fizzle sensation jolted across the roof of her mouth and her tongue, she realised she was getting a numb feeling in her hands and feet. Before long she realised she couldn't move, only her eyes were able to move, she couldn't speak. Glancing

at the empty cup on the table.
 Had she been drugged?
There was a loud click and the door opened, Richard stood there with his hands on his hips.
"Perfect timing" he smiled with achievement.
Richard walked over to her, towering over her and looked down.
"You are an outsider here, you don't understand do you?"
He scratched his head. "Florence is a staple to this town, she showed us the way, his way."
Richard smiled again, this time with a demonic expression behind his eyes and showed his full set of perfectly white teeth.
"Now she is going to show you the way too"
Richard grabbed her by the feet and dragged her through the corridor when there was another voice from over towards a desk.
"Lively one Rich?"
A deep voice boomed.
 Sam couldn't see him as she couldn't turn her head as she led on the floor staring at poster that said "We are here for you"
"This one is a troublemaker"
Richard replied and they both laughed with a manic tone.
Dragged out of the front door, she was on her stomach.
Yanked across the concrete driveway, she was numb from pain. She left a trail of blood behind her.
Arms hugged around her stomach as she was lifted and pushed into the back of a car, Richard quickly got into the driver's seat

and turned the key in the ignition. The car roared to life as vibration jolted the back seats that Sam led on.

With nothing but the back of the black leather seats in her view, Sam listened to the sounds of the car, occasionally the sound of the gearbox nearly stalling it and the hub on one of the tyres was rattling away near her head.

Street lights were passing over the car as they shone lights over the back of the seats and Richard was saying nothing on the drive which seemed to last forever. The car slowed down and the sound of gravel stones erupted from below.

Sam gulped, absolute fear crossed her mind because she knew she was back at the house.

The car engine stopped and the sound of the handbrake gave her a slight jumpscare, she still couldn't move.

The sound of gravel under feet came closer and closer, the car door opened and that recognisable horrendous voice emerged.

"Oh good, Richard you brought her back to me"

It was the voice of Miss Parr of course, pulling Sam back to the land of the living.

"Of course, we'll need her later I assume"

Richard opened the back door by Sam's feet, pulled at them and Sam slid out and onto the gravel, still no pain.

She was now looking at the sky, it was pitch plank with a hue of purple thick clouds, there were no stars in sight.

Miss Parr's face came into vision overhead, looking down at her with snake-like eyes.

"You are a nasty little one aren't you?"

She leered at Sam as her eyes were slightly glowing with an

orange hue, Richard was now looking over her with the same coloured eyes.

"I told her, she'll know his way soon enough"

Richard smiled and looked at Miss Parr.

"I am afraid that this one will never understand,"

"Please take her to the outhouse Richard, the others are mostly gone but there's a few stragglers that will watch over her"

Dragged across the gravel by her feet again. The familiar smell of the musty house came back with a vengeance. Still lit with candles. It projected an eerie flickering glow onto the ceiling.

Then along the stone floor of the glass corridor, she remembered Artemis was guarding and had a fear that it would go for her jugular, but he didn't seem to be around anymore.

Into the courtyard and through to the outhouse, she came through the door to an unfamiliar room. She saw the feet of the chairs and realised she was in the room where everybody was watching the murder take place.

Left aside a few steps, she noticed blood still dripping from the altar above her. The wood seemed to absorb the red drops. A small grey hand lay drooped over the side of the altar.

"Richard, well done"

A man's voice, definitely much older.

"Thanks, just doing my job!"

Richard said in a humorous and sarcastic tone and the door closed, believing Richard to have now left the room.

She felt a breath on her ear, but she couldn't see what it was.

She smelt something sweet. It was the breath of someone up close, there was a deep inhale through the nose of her hair that made her feel disgusted. The person had now moved away and Sam felt relieved thinking the horror could have at that moment become something else entirely.
A conversation then erupted.
"We bring them in from all over really" This was a familiar manly voice, she instantly recognised it and it took a few minutes to realize it was the driver.
"Florence and I have connections, you see. It's a completely endless resource, these… people are not missed, we are able to cross a few boxes and then the paperwork goes missing, a few people sign it off and there you go" he laughed amongst a group of people.
"Well, it serves the entire town doesn't it? This town will never experience the yobs, the immigrants, the chaos that other places experience because we are here to protect it" this was a sweet softer voice and Sam couldn't believe she was hearing such a casual conversation.
"His reach is growing, Moloch's wisdom will reshape the fabric of society one town at a time" this was another voice, it sounded posh and very distinctive, almost a royal quality.
Sam at this moment had realised that she had found her way into a cult. And Miss Parr was just a piece of the puzzle, the whole town was in on this. She was still staring at the lifeless hand and wondered where his parents had been, *why couldn't they help their child?*

23

THE NIGHT BEFORE

"Noah, wait!" a voice cried out into the dark misty woods, lit by the high sitting moon above. "Noah, slow down!" the voice continued echoing and bouncing off the thin creaking trees. Noah and Charlie were out late on Halloween, this was against the wish of their Father, but he was out cold drunk at home when they left.

The child ahead, Noah was the youngest of the two boys, he was twelve and had bright blonde hair that sat swept to the side and at medium length, he was a thin boy that wore dark blue jeans and an american baseball style jacket. He was running through the woods with a large stick, bashing the trees as he ran, making lightsaber sounds from his favourite movie. Trying to keep up was Charlie, the eldest brother was overweight for his age of fifteen. His short brown hair damp with sweat, and his grey baggy t-shirt had dark patches too. He wiped dirt from his hands onto his jeans, as he kept falling onto his palms.

When Charlie caught up with his brother, they were now both staring at the House in the distance, a dark red glow illuminating the back half of the house and the moonlight on the other side.

"We can't go near there No, You know what's in there!" No

was short for Noah, only Charlie called him that. "I don't believe in Vampires" laughed the small boy as he swung his stick at his brother.
"Cut it out!"
An owl hoots and flies overhead, the trees are rustling in the slight breeze and there is a distant sound of wind chimes followed by the low roar of what Charlie thought was a large cat that was originating from the nearby zoo.
"No, we should have been back home ten minutes ago"
Noah walked across a fallen tree, he stretched his arms out as he walked it like a tightrope, the worn oak creaked beneath his Nike trainers.
"You know Dad is just blind drunk again anyway, we could be out here all night and he'll not notice we are still out" Noah tried balancing on one foot before quickly wobbling and using his other foot again to steady him.
The woodland cleared away to an open field next to the house, Charlie realized they had drifted ever closer to it. It seemed to be drawing them in, Charlie thought to himself It's like a tractor beam or a spell.
"What ya mean you don't believe in Vampires?"
Charlie chuckled as he grabbed Noah by the back of his jacket. "They'll catch you and turn you into one of them!" Charlie growled in an over the top creepy and croaky voice.
"You are so dumb" Noah waved his arm which knocked his brother's hand away from him.
Charlie and Noah lost their mother months ago. She collapsed at home, and doctors were perplexed. How she died is still

unknown.

Plagued by nightmares of his mother. Appearing at Charlie's window at night. So often that he started sticking plasters in the shape of crucifixes, to his window pane. He became obsessed with Vampires, probably because his Dad would sit and watch *Salem's Lot, Dracula* and *The Lost Boys* on rotation for weeks on end.

There was the sound of a snapping twig from the dark tree line they just walked away from, and the wind had slowly begun to pick up its strength as it began to blow through the leaves of the trees. It created a whirlwind mini tornado of dead leaves across the damp grass, of which was shining in the moonlight.

"What was that?" Noah was rarely scared, even as the younger brother.

"I told you, we need to go home" Charlie sounded tired and fed up now of his little brother's inability to listen to him.

There was a slight whisper from between the trees where darkness seemed to stir. Charlie fixed his eyes on something, maybe an outline but the lighting made it impossible to work out what he was looking at, but he felt a chill creep over him. Charlie walked towards the tree line, his brother was talking about something, but he had completely blocked him out and it was just background noise to him now. He walked into the treeline to the sound of his brother now shouting

"Charlie, where are you going?"

The wind fell still, and Charlie was swallowed by the darkness between the swaying trees.

"Charlie stop playing around, i know you are going to jump

out at me" Throwing his stick into the treeline with a snapping sound as it bounced off a tree. There was no response, until the stick came hurtling back, nearly hitting him at full speed. "Charlie! What the hell!" Noah was angry now.

Walking towards the treeline himself, he felt a dread he had never felt before, he felt like there were a million eyes on him, and then wind once again began to stir around him, leaves smashed against his jacket and then broke loose as they floated through the air.

It happened very quickly and he didn't see any trace of his brother. What he did find was the black shadow of a large hand reach over his face, and he was cold just like that.

24

PRESENT DAY

A tingling sensation began to trickle through Sam's toes—she was starting to feel something again. But with the return of sensation came dread. She would soon feel the pain flood her body, from the wounds left by being dragged such a great distance.

She kept her eyes fixed on the lifeless hand nearby, which had finally stopped dripping blood onto the floor.

"Get your hands off me!" shouted a younger voice—a boy's, high and cracking under the strain of puberty and rage.

Sam managed to turn her head slightly. A fairly overweight teenager stood struggling, a nasty gash splitting his forehead. "Noah!" he cried, his gaze locking on the body lying beside Sam on the altar. "What did you do to him?!"

"Quiet, lad!" barked the driver, striking the boy with the back of his hand. The boy whimpered and sobbed.

Sam's body ignited with pain—hot, sharp, like flames licking her skin. The tingling needles crawling up her back were unbearable, but she managed to wriggle on the floor.

"She's coming to," said a voice from the back of the room. It belonged to a hooded figure—one of many standing in the shadows, silently observing.

"What… is wrong with you people?" Sam croaked, her words dragging out through clenched teeth.

"We are the future," the robed figures chanted in eerie unison. Into a back room, Charlie was dragged behind a curtain. Sam never saw or heard from him again. The worst clawed at her mind.

With great effort, Sam sat up. Pain flared from her shoulder blades down to her lower back, making her wince. She tasted blood in her mouth, warm and metallic. Instinctively, she swallowed, but it made her stomach twist in discomfort. Her arms were covered in scratches and blooming bruises. A deep cut on her shin had torn through her jeans.

Two of the hooded figures approached. One of them carried a length of frayed rope. Sam had no strength left to resist.

Within moments, they had tied her up. Placed behind her back, bamboo sticks were twisted into the rope to cinch it further—leaving no room to squirm.

Sam was past tears. Now there was only rage.

They're not taking me. Not like this.

No one paid her any further attention. The robed figures stood in scattered groups, whispering to one another like guests at a wedding reception—or a funeral wake. In the corner, a suitcase record player crackled softly with classical music. It sounded familiar, though Sam couldn't name the piece.

Then the grandfather clock chimed.

Miss Parr appeared, her expression unreadable. She motioned silently, guiding the robed figures through the door and into the courtyard. She didn't smile, didn't speak. Just a nod for each as they vanished into the night.
Grasping Sam's arm the most violent way, flinging her onto her feet like a rag doll, Miss Parr was speaking in another language, a language she heard nights ago when she was hiding under the kitchen table.
Bound by rope, it was already causing sores on her wrists. The more she tried to wiggle, the more it rubbed and burnt her skin.
Back to the house under watchful eye. They passed Artemis in the hall, this time there was no low growl. Sam had been caught and was pleased with it.
As they opened the doors into the reception area. The candles flickered in unison, bending to the devil's will before slowly returning to normal.
Miss Parr smiled from ear to ear and rubbed her palms together that displayed a hint of celebration.
They were now in the first floor corridor, Miss Parr unlocked a door to reveal darkness and swung Sam through the open door, sending her to the floor with a painful thud as the floorboards sounded like they cracked out of place beneath her.
"You can lock me up in here, but you are running out of ways to scare me, your parlour tricks are just that, silly tricks" Sam

snapped, she was angry now and Miss Parr sensed a new sense of energy from her, a fire she overlooked.

"There are no tricks in this house, only the guardians, and the spirits of those that came before you" Sam couldn't see her expression, her silhouette stood tall in the doorway and then vanished with the door slamming to.

The room was dark, but it wasn't as pitch black as Sam had expected it to be, not like the room where the dolls slept. Newspaper blocked out the window, and bars contained a fireplace. She scoped the room, looking for options of escape. She tried to use the corner of the windowsill to tear the rope or loosen it, but that didn't work, it just further rubbed against her wounds.

The room was empty of furniture like many of the other rooms she had seen, but there was a half height bookcase in the corner.

Tap..Tap..Tap

Pausing to listen, Sam could hear the tapping noises again. She could even feel it through the floor beneath her feet, it continued to tap, almost like morse code, but she didn't know how that worked.

The tapping stopped when she placed her foot over a floorboard that was a different shade of colour, it seemed out of place. Sam slowly dropped to the ground and tried to use her hands behind her back to lift the board as it was loose. But it was too difficult. Her fingers traced around the edge of the board, trying to find grip. She then kicked the board with her heel, the first attempt did nothing.

The second attempt just hurt her heel, as pain travelled up the back of her leg.

Her heel came crashing down, it dropped the board down on one side. A bent and rusty nail jolted up into the air. She tried to use this to break the rope, but she couldn't do it with her arms behind her back.

The tapping continued again, noticing something under the boards, she reluctantly pushed herself down through the gap, conscious that she was inches from scraping herself on the blunt nail, she couldn't see anything in the small space beneath the boards.

After some struggle Sam got back to her feet and walked towards the door, she tried to release the rope with the door handle, it kept flinging back into place and was not giving her the leverage she needed.

Sam had an idea, she tugged at the floorboard with it between her legs, she kept pulling and pulling and eventually it came to and was now between her legs and away from the floor. She pushed across the other side of the room with her feet towards the window and turned her back to it, squatted down and grabbed it with her hands. Lifting the wood up behind her back she placed it resting against the window and then began to kick it up with her feet, it fell down to the floor the first three attempts, each time more frustrating than the last.

With a click on the fourth attempt, there was a chinkling of glass, she had managed to crack the glass with the weight of the board against it, she continued to hit the board over and over again until the glass finally smashed.

She waited several moments before she took any further action, expecting Miss Parr to burst in, but it never occurred to her surprise, but then the house was big enough to mask the sound of a simple glass smashing.

Sam used a shard of glass to cut away the rope, it was working but it was a slow process, swapping out for another sharper piece a few times, her hands were bleeding but it was worth the struggle. Blood trickled down her hands and dripped onto the dusty boards below.

The rope was fraying, but Sam was beginning to sense something in the room with her. She didn't want to wait and see what was about to reveal itself and continued to frantically cut at the rope, her shoulder blades beginning to now ache.

The air around her began to thicken, something was stirring in the corner of the room. There was a twisting of shapes from the side of her vision, she turned her back to it and continued to cut away, faster and faster.

There was a ticking sound that was edging closer, it was the ticking of a clock, it was right behind her head now and it was ticking faster and faster. She had to look now, there was no avoiding it, as she peered over her shoulder slowly, there was a grandfather clock, but it was moving like a tall human, its body had a pendant ticking left to right, it had huge outstretching arms made from wood panelling, and its face was a shining gold, a clock with black eyes and yellow teeth and it began to sing.

Hickory, dickory, dock
The mouse ran up the clock.
The clock struck one
The mouse ran down
Hickory, dickory, dock.

The figure opened its mouth wider and wider as a wave of white mice came flowing out, they ran up Sam's legs and arms and were completely submerging her. The clock figure had disappeared, but it was still laughing with a menacing fade into the darkness.
The mice had vanished not long after they had quickly appeared, Sam couldn't breathe, she was hyperventilating as a cold sweat was erupting all over her body. She could make sense of the other encounters in the house, but this one was twisted, it made no sense, it didn't seem human in any way.
In the moment she had realised she had cut herself free from the rope, she had a piece still tied tight around her wrists but this didn't bother her too much.
The door was locked, there was no chance Miss Parr would make that mistake.
Moments before the clock figure had tormented Sam. Florence sat on her knees, in front of a small table. Dressed with a black cloth, and had incense burning along with tea lights scattered around it. The thin trail of smoke twisted, and turned in the air. She enjoyed the opium scent, which was delightful to her

sense of smell, as her eyes were resting shut.

"Moloch waits with burning eyes,
 Underneath the ashen skies.
 Bones to dust and fire to coal,
 Feed the flame, forsake the soul.

She raises her arms up beside her, with her index finger and thumb touching, creating symbolic gestures.

Moloch, Moloch, horned and high,
 Hear our plea, devour the sky.
 Blood for breath and breath for bone,
 Claim the child, claim the throne.

The candles violently flickered, and quickly extinguished as the room fell dark. Triggering a viciously wide smile from Florence as she had felt a vile presence enter the house. Picking up Artemis from her side with a hand underneath him, holding him in place, she stroked his head softly, he purred and his eyes squinted in bliss.

25

TWO YEARS AGO

The money was worth it.
Florence stood aside a gaping abyss. The sun beating down on the Ferrule of her umbrella, which was slung over her shoulder. Egypt had been enlightening for her. It had taken a lot of research to find the spot where various workers were still hard at work, uncovering the tomb entrance.
The workers didn't stop to wipe the sweat from their bare chests, they were all topless in the haze of the intense heat. cloth around their heads, most of them having beards filled with grains of sand. They shouted an unfamiliar language at each other, Florence's gaze was fixed on them, watching them above like a hawk. She had caught one of them earlier that day, upon discovering an ancient coin they had tried to stuff it into their pockets as extra payment.
Florence had spent a significant amount of money on the dig. It would be quite possible, and not unlikely, they would never find what she was looking for out here, it was at best a myth. She searched for Moloch's tomb, believing the ancient texts she had studied (and many before her) led people to believe it was a bull-headed figure, but this always led to nothing of significance.

It was her personal encounter that had led her on the correct path, in the flames she had sprung in the mansion house many years before, encountering the great black owl that swooped over her; it haunted her nightmares for many years that followed.

Upon further research, she found that a secret society amongst the powerful, rich and famous.

Founded in eighteen seventy eight, it belonged to a private club, known as the Bohemian Club. annually and at the height of summer, the Bohemian Grove hosted some of the most powerful people in the world.

Particularly famous for a planning meeting that took place there in the nineteen forties, which led to the creation of the atomic bomb.

The Cremation of Care ceremony was a theatrical performance in which the club's members participated. Usually someone playing the High Priest. And it was described as an exorcising of the Demon. The ceremony took place in front of the Owl Shrine of Moloch. The moss covered statue from afar looks akin to natural rock, yet holds a monitoring station within. A recording of a voice of a club member was used as the voice of The Owl during the ceremony.

Florence had travelled out to California in the previous summer. She found herself a way into the club with her unique abilities to commune with the dead. She quickly became a well regarded club member and often played the High Priest in the ceremony.

This is where she learned the importance of sacrifice. Children were offered up as sacrifices to Moloch during the ceremony. They were made up of children who were missing, or lost in the system. Mostly they were children who were being trafficked.

All of her research had led to this day in the blistering heat, the sand blowing around her feet and all of the disturbance led to scorpions rising from the depths of the dune sea.

This tomb would be of significance, it would help her cause in spreading the truth of Moloch and the teachings, and growing the influence.

One of the workers swung his steel pickaxe at the red stone that blocked an entrance way. With a hiss and clanking mechanical sound flames had erupted from cracks in the stone walls. The workers were now engulfed, screaming and flesh burning. Florence realized the significance of the flame trap, it was said in the scriptures that Moloch's followers would ensure the unclean would meet flame.

Flesh burned away and bubbled at the exposed flesh, it fell away in large chunks from their bones as it slopped down onto the sand below, cooking like a rib-eye steak in the sunlight. Florence cut a dark and sinister smile as she handed her umbrella to the worker next to her, he stood with a terrified expression, as he watched his crew take their last breath.

The flames had shifted the rocks and had retreated back into the dark crevices of the ancient walls. Florence felt the presence of the guardians with her, guiding her into the dark tomb.

The tomb was not large, it would be considered by many to be quite claustrophobic. This didn't phase Florence at all.

As she entered the room, flames ignited the torches that rested in steel cages on the walls. It revealed the ancient carvings and glyphs on the walls, covering every inch of stone.

Great owl statues faced each other on each side, guarding a large stone tomb.

"Aperire Angelis"

Florence uttered these words in a hiss-like whisper, almost speaking in tongues could be described. The ground trembled as the tomb slid aside to reveal a spiral staircase going further down. A breeze erupted from the depths, followed by a distant tortured group of screams, quite similar to the sound the worker men had sounded upon their flesh melting ends. There was a smell, a blend of rotting meat, sour milk, feces, and a sharp, sickly sweet mysterious undertone. Even this smell made Florence wretch.

She made her way deeper, pacing down the spiral staircase into the blackness below. Light erupted in front of her upon reaching the bottom. It revealed another small space, this time a pool of dark water sat in the middle of the chamber, beyond that there was a great owl statue, a smaller version of the one found at Bohemian Grove.

Glyphs on the walls had shown everything that had already happened on earth, and everything that was going to happen before Moloch's return. There were images of political leaders, faceless children being thrown into flames and a woman figure that strikingly looked like Florence herself.

She stepped into the murky stagnant pool, it was warm but felt gritty on her feet and ankles, she could feel pieces of something floating amongst it, some were mossy while others were feather-like.

"In sanguine tuo cum devotione lavo" she spoke again, confidently, the words she learnt from the ancient scriptures. Old Latin translates i bathe in your blood with commitment. Something shone beneath the water, a small red object that she lifted in her palm, she twisted it within her fingers, it was reflectively beautiful, it had many crystals encrusted deep within it's rock like structure, and while it looked heavy, it was impressively light.

Smiling, she slipped it into her pocket and made her way out of the pool that swirled around her feet. She made her way back up the spiral staircase and out of the chamber into the sunlight, instantly feeling a burning sensation across the skin of her arms.

A man stood waiting, he was in an all black and expensive suit, he wore dark rounded sunglasses and a black trilby shaped hat. Upon glancing at Florence he smiled, revealing a large gap in his front teeth.

"You find what you were looking for?" he said as he waved one of the workers to leave them.

"I did, and now we can proceed, I know of a place where we will not draw any unwanted attention"

"What is our destination?" The man now sucked on a thick and rather expensive cigar.

"England"

The cigar man and Florence climbed the camels handed to them, swaying amongst the charred body parts that lay amongst the shifting sands. They vanished into the mirage of the desert heat.

26

THREE MONTHS PRIOR

Florence sat in a large, comfortable green leather armchair amongst the many books of her library. Studying a large glossy black book, it had nothing on the cover, it was purely reflective and the book contained many scribbles and drawings of strange symbols.

She had invited many people from the town along to the house. Now with Violet out of the picture, she had some time. Deciding it was time to bend the will of more townsfolk.

The compound was ready, it could be extracted from the blood when at the point of death or extreme torment.. But from the age of puberty this compound would begin to weaken.

You could inject, ingest, or rub this compound into your skin, preserving life and preventing aging. This of course allowed Florence to look how she did, when she was not far from turning one hundred and two years old.

Ilfracombe was an ageing town, but it was also a town in which the prison population would receive its worst offenders. It wasn't a place to raise a family like it once was. And so began the rise of a cult that began to take leadership across the town.

Florence sought to bring them into her congregation, much to the residents' delight, they were able to live on with this compound at the expense of sacrificing the young.

Children would go missing all over Devonshire, between 1997 and 2003 there were 25 missing children. Eventually it led to outside interference looking into the missing person cases and so Florence had to find a new alternative.

Meeting Peter, a fellow devotee to Moloch, who drove for many institutions from carting around the rich and famous, to politicians and everyone in between, he was able to find his way into the care system and with a few strings here and there, they had the perfect plan to take the Children off the books and into the arms of Florence.

Florence's personal motivations were simple, she had grown a hatred for the normal person due to her upbringing. She believed the race of Molochians were the evolution of the human race. Believing that they would eventually outnumber them and take complete control.

There were those that opposed her, for one the captain of the local force Micky, he had been a policeman in Ilfracombe since the sixties and had seen the slow disappearance of nice folk across town.

Florence sipped her tea, taking in the minty flavour she had added to the brew. She observed the symbols in the pages of the book, tracing them with her fingers as if she was learning to speak them. Artemis sat on the arm rest beside her watching out into the library's dusty essence. Spears of light pierced through the tatty curtains that hung on the tall windows that overlooked the field of horses.

Her mind turned a corner as she thought about Micky again, it had been a while since she had that kind of conflict with someone else. Normally she would scare anybody into submission with her dark arts, but Micky was stubborn.

27

A YEAR PRIOR

Micky was sitting at the wheel of his panda car, his daughter loved to call it that, and that made him smile whenever he thought of it.
Micky was a short balding man, slightly podgy around the waist much to the disappointment of his doctor. He wore large specs that his wife would mock him for being a spitting image of Dennis Taylor, which of course annoyed Micky but he loved Snooker too so it wasn't so bad. That was his other love, he would spend his evenings down the snooker hall in the eighties, but that had long since closed down. Now he had to resort to playing Pool on a tatty old table in the Grand Harbour pub.
He used to be a policeman in *Barnstaple*, the neighbouring town. It was more populated and had a higher crime rate. Since being transferred to *Ilfracombe*, he had become complacent with his work and often left the small petty crimes for Richard to deal with.
Richard sat in the passenger seat, he was chowing down on a Greggs sausage roll and crumbs fell onto his lap. They were parked just tucked away to the side of *Oxford Grove*, a place where the local druggies would meet. Drugs that had increased in circulation in the last few weeks, *Ilfracombe* always had its pot heads and meth addicts, but there was a new drug going

around that seemed to be spreading like wildfire. Micky had arrested an elderly man in the harbour pub the previous night, he found him down an alleyway injecting it into his arm. All the way back to the station the man was smiling on a high and said nothing.

"You see that old woman that's taken the old mansion?" Richard wasn't looking at Micky while saying this, his eyes fixed on the entrance of the car park like he was expecting a gang of armed thugs to appear. Micky loved his enthusiasm but it was a bit much at times, he thought Richard was watching too many American action movies.

"No? I am surprised anyone would want to live in that place, it gives me the creeps, I remember when I was about fifteen years old and I snuck in there with my girlfriend at the time Tracey-" just as he said her name Richard turned his head with a smile and of complete surprise.

"Wait, Tracey Dougan?" he nearly choked on his Sausage Roll at this stage.

"Yeah, alright, she was a looker back then yer know?" Micky was not having it, he remembered her when she had long legs, flowing blonde hair and bright blue eyes. Now she looked more like a cross between a womble and..well, melted ice cream.

"I can't believe that, Tracey, good looking? Fuck" Richard was laughing as more crumbs from his pastry broke off.

The radio gave a static hiss as voices broke through "Micky, there's a bunch of little bastards throwing stones at the Sunspot arcade again" said a gruff female voice. "Thanks Trish, we'll check it out" Micky replied.

"Well?" Richard was looking at Micky with anticipation.

"Well what?"

"You snuck into the mansion with the bimbo?" Richard was excited at the prospect of an interesting story.

"Oh! Well, yeah i am not sure what it was i saw, but it was evil, i remember glowing eyes, and a stretched out hand towards me" Micky paused, his eyes were glazed over as he was back in his fifteen year old mind. "Yeah I saw something.." he said as his fingers touched the top of the steering wheel.

The atmosphere changed in the car, but was quickly broken by Richard's sense of humour.

"Cmon ghosts really?" he laughed as he threw his napkin at Micky's face.

"You laugh boy but this town has its fair share, now cmon lets go see about these little shits."

They pulled away and drove down the steep hill towards town, it was bustling as it was peak summer season, which is most likely why kids were playing up and causing trouble. The local kids hated the summer because it was full of strange folk from out of town looking for a cheap getaway and the kids didn't have school either.

"Look! Slow down, there she is Mick" Richard pointed at the passing street, Miss Parr was on the pavement walking through the crowd of bucket hats, sunscreen and swimming trunks. She stuck out like a sore thumb in a long velvet red coat and black netted hat.

"You know, I think she lived in that house years ago, there was a family that died up there in a fire, it's a wonder they were able to restore the place" Mick remembered her face, once belonging to a younger girl of course but something about her stuck in his memory.

They sped up down the road and turned the corner towards the signs for Tunnels Beaches, the quickest route to the arcade from the high street. Not far from the destination sat another arcade, this one was burnt out and closed down, on the left next to the museum. They were certain at the time it was an insurance job, but fires were always popping up somewhere in *Ilfracombe.*

"There they are" Richard pointed across the road, there were a bunch of hooded kids no older than thirteen, huddled around outside the theatre, one of which was smoking what seemed to be a very large spliff. The theatre is just one of the strangest additions to the town, locals called it Madonna's Bra because of two large cone structures on top of the building.

They pulled up on the double yellows (perks of the job) and they both almost in sync, got out of the car and slowly walked over to the group. "James, what a surprise, it's always you, where's yer dad?" Micky was looking at a scrawny kid with short brown unkempt hair and a stud through his left earlobe.

"What u gonna arrest me man?" he said with an attitude that just wasn't going to intimidate them.

Richard loomed over the boy with serious eyes.

"Maybe we should dump you over the cliff, it would do

everybody a favour" Richard was dead pan and lifeless behind the eyes.

"What the – Richard, back off i'll deal with them" Micky was pissed off with Richard, he couldn't believe what he had said to him, James was a little bastard for sure but, threatening him like that was not acceptable by anyone let alone a police officer.

"Man's fuckin crazy, i'll tell my old man about this!" another coloured boy stepped out from the group with his chest puffed out as the other boys laughed.

Micky took the lit spliff from the boy's mouth, stubbed it out on the floor under his boot and then crushed it in his palm. After a short but more constructive conversation the boys moved on, they always do in the end.

The two men walked over towards the sunspot arcade to speak with the owner and check for any damage to the glass doors.

"Richard, what the hell was that about?" Micky was concerned.

"What? Oh come on Mick, sometimes you just have to scare these kids a little" he smirked while lifting his palms in the air and giving a passive shrug.

"No, I don't want you doing that kinda thing again, we're not a mob, were police officers" Micky waved his finger at Richard and moved in front and through the doors.

They had a long discussion with the owner of the arcade, he'd been running it since Micky could ever remember and now business was booming since the other arcade and competition had burned down.

There was a creepy machine there that Micky hated, as a small boy his father would scare him with just the thought of it, it was a dummy like character, very classic looking that you would expect to see on the lap of a ventriloquist. It would sit lifeless until you pushed in a twenty pence coin and it would suddenly burst out in song and dance.

They're changing guard at Buckingham Palace -
Christopher Robin went down with Alice.
Alice is marrying one of the guard.
"A soldier's life is terrible hard,"
Says Alice.

Micky stood next to the machine, the doll was encased with glass as it stood drooped over and lifeless, waiting for the next poor soul to insert the coin and wake him up, which Micky would not think to even contemplate.

As the evening approached and the sun began to fall behind the cliffs, a call came into the station from Miss Parr. She was complaining about a group of kids that matched the same description as James and the others from earlier that day. Micky sent Richard to disperse them and several hours had passed before he returned.
He was looking rather pale and sweaty, Micky thought Richard must have been coming down with something and that was the reason behind his strange comments earlier in the day.

"Are you OK?" Micky was sitting at his desk, arms folded and leaning back on his chair on its two back legs.
"Yeah, i am just tired" Richard rubbed his eyes and then the back of his neck.
"Well lets clock off for today, i'll be on call, you can rest up, maybe avoid the beer tonight aye?" chuckled Micky as they both left the station and drove away in separate cars.

It was the early hours, around one thirty in the morning according to Micky's digital clock that sat next to his bed, the red lined digits reflecting in his eyes. His long distance walkie had hissed, or at least he was dreaming that it did.
Moments passed with no further noise, he was certain it was what woke him up and his eyes slowly began to drop when he was startled by the other hiss of the radio.
"Mick?" the voice said.
Mick spun his legs out of the bed and was now hanging off the edge, he was in white and blue striped pyjamas and his wife was snoring beside him.
"Who's on this line?" he was whispering but also shouting, trying to be discreet but it was never Micky's strongest skill. Micky was asking this because they would normally call his landline at home, Richard had a walkie on this frequency and the other tuned in radio was back at the station.
"Capstone" is all Micky could make out next amongst the hiss of the radio, Capstone? This was the name of the hill that sat on the beachfront, and now he was concerned that someone had fallen over the edge. He waited for further instruction but

after five minutes there was no further communication.
He decided to get dressed, not in his uniform though, he was on call but there was no chance he was going to get into all his gear at this time. It was very unusual to be called out unless there was a fight somewhere at one of the drinking holes in town.

28

Micky drove a little faster than usual through the deserted dark high street, there was no one around and no other cars either. As he approached Sunspot Amusements and Capstone Hill, it was eerie and still, he expected to see Richard there perhaps looking concerned, maybe some family members of someone missing but there was no one.
Parking up by the clapping circle, he left his car door open and walked towards the centre of the circle, it was quite the hidden landmark. If you clapped in the centre of the circle it would cause a high pitched whistle alongside, created by the acoustics of the surrounding area. The kids at school used to say that if you clapped three times the ghost of a pirate would appear and try to behead you. But no one ever claimed to actually see it.
Micky looked up towards the flagpole on the hill, the union jack flag was very still as the sea remained calm that night. The salt air was fresh through Micky's nostrils that were partially blocked with an oncoming cold as he listened for any sounds other than the low crashing waves on the grey pebble beach.
Just preparing to turn around and go home, he noticed a small light on top of the hill. It was very brief but it seemed like a

lantern or maybe the flame of a lighter. He stood waiting for it to reappear, his eyes fixed on the area where he saw it. After moments passed he was going to call it there and head back but as he did he saw the light again, it was flickering manically in the darkness like a will-o-wisp.

Micky intently began to walk towards the foot of the hill, it was dark and there was not much light up there, so he had to be careful not to misstep. They did have solar lights on the walkway but it seemed some of them went missing and some of them just stopped working and were never replaced.

Halfway up the steep hill, he looked back over his shoulder to see the majority of the town in view, it wrapped itself up towards the tree line on the horizon, but you couldn't see past the rooftop of the school. There were only a few houses with lights on at this time.

Continuing up the hill, he realised he didn't feel alone anymore, he felt someone was watching him now. There was a small opening in the hill where a man made alcove and a bench sat. If there was anyone here it would be right at that spot, normally Pete would be there, everyone knew him as he was just one of three homeless people that lived there and often slept on that bench, but he died In the winter just passed.

The bench sat empty.

Scratching his head and looking around him, Micky had no idea exactly where the light he saw had actually come from. "Hello?" he called out, not afraid to be shouting as he was not

close to any houses right now, he heard his own voice through an echo.
Now walking up to the flagpole, it was surrounded in a tiny metal fence to stop kids from shaking at the pole and dislodging it from the ground. He called out again, this time quite nervously as he felt watched again.
"Is there anyone up here, are you OK? Police" making himself not only known but also it made him feel safer as he projected his authority out into the dark night. He realised how dark it really was, but also how clear the night was too. The sky was lit by a million white lights, perhaps this is why he felt watched, he felt vulnerable underneath so much space.
He heard a whisper in front of him, only just a few yards away but it sent shivers down his spine, his teeth clattered together with an icy chill at the words he was hearing.
"They're changing guard at Buckingham Palace"
Followed by a high pitched giggle.

Micky's heart was thumping in his neck and through his ears. He thought it might be someone playing a trick, but then to realise that anyone that would know he was scared of that damn singing dummy, were either dead or lived thousands of miles away. He never told Richard or anyone at the station of this silly fear, which is what he felt it was.
His skeptical mind took control of the situation.
"Alright, come on out now, i won't ask again" he shouted, his voice bellowing across the rocky terrain that sharply dropped on the other side of the hill. He moved towards the edge and

looked over, it was dark but the starlit sky did reveal the jagged rocks and the ocean waves that crashed beneath him.

It was a long way down.

"Christopher Robin went down with Alice."
The voice had erupted again, this time not a whisper but a low level voice and what terrified him the most was that it sounded just like that dummy in the glass box. It came from directly behind him and close by.

He began to doubt himself, did he tell anyone in the pub one night after a few ale's? Well it was quite possible.

Without any warning or anyone in view, Micky felt a crushing pain in his ribs, a burning shove on him with enough force to cause him to fall backwards, he tried to grapple anything he could, but with no success. He had no time to even scream as his body plummeted to the rocks below like a ragdoll. Micky had vanished within the depths of the sea.

29

PRESENT DAY

Sam peeked through newspaper clippings that covered the broken window. She had punched a hole through it to get her bearings in the house. She had a shard of glass ready in her hand, wrapped in a strip of t-shirt that she had ripped. Thinking about her escape plan when the door opened next, she didn't care now if she was to attack Miss Parr. It was her best option for surviving.
Would she go for the jugular? Sam didn't want to kill anybody, not even Miss Parr.
If she didn't, she risked being killed herself.. Like the boy on the altar with his throat slit.
Trying the door handle again, perhaps some miracle had unlocked the door since her last attempt, she had already seen ghosts and monsters in the house so anything was possible.
Perhaps Violet could open the door.
She realised that someone was standing on the other side, she heard footsteps marching past, left then right, like they were on guard and were too loud to be Artemis.
"Who's there?"
There was no response but the footsteps did suddenly stop

after her voice had travelled through the crack in the door.
"Look" whispered a voice
Sam quickly fell to her knees and peeked through the keyhole but there was nothing, just the darkness of the hallway beyond.
Standing back on her feet she pulled at the door with all her strength, the wood creaked and groaned but it wasn't budging at all.
"Look" the voice repeated again, with a slight giggle this time, but not of a child's voice.
She dropped to her knees, this time hesitantly looked through. She held her sight for a moment, looking back at her was another eye. She fell backwards in terror, even if it was someone that could help her, it had frightened Sam.
There was a small laugh and then the footsteps of someone running away.
Reaching breaking point, Sam wrapped her arms around her legs and curled herself tight, her hand still grasping the shard of glass, she sunk her head down and started to sob, tears running down her cheeks and dropping onto her exposed stomach where she had ripped the t-shirt.
At this stage she was feeling helpless, she had lost all hope of getting out of the house. She began to wonder what exactly was real and what was in her head.
The door swung open and Miss Parr barrelled into the room, she instantly noticed the broken window and her face turned a violent dark red. It seemed like she was already a step ahead and fully expected the next move from Sam.

Still woozy from the drugs earlier, Sam lurched forward with her hand in the air, grasping the shard of glass, her eyes were wild, she knew she couldn't hold back at this moment if she was to escape. Miss Parr punched at her forearm, it didn't knock the makeshift blade from her hand though as she swiped again at Miss Parr's midsection, which she had narrowly avoided by sucking in her stomach and arching her back. A violent slap was thrown with Miss Parr's other hand as it crashed across Sam's cheek, leaving a dark red mark that would definitely be leaving a bruise.

This just made Sam more rage induced and she swung again aimlessly this time, it tore a neat line on Miss Parr's shoulder and blood had quickly begun to drip down her arm. Sam left no time to waste and swung again, slashing at her thigh and causing a similar wound.

Miss Parr clutched at her thigh and almost howled like a wolf in pain. Her eyes fixed on her wound at first. danced over to Sam again and were locked in.

"Let me go, now" Sam was pointing the blood soaked glass fang at her with a new found confidence.

Miss Parr, like a creature hunched over, had wiped her blood soaked hand over her chin. now had it smeared on her face as she exposed her janky teeth. It was in this moment that Sam realised she was almost not human, whatever she had managed to do with her herbs and potions over the years had made her something else. Her eyes glowing orange and her face crooked and wrinkled up with absolute rage, her stance mimicked that of a werewolf.

Pointing the sharp glass at her, Sam moved closer and nearly touched her neck as she slowly guided herself to the door. She knew that one wrong calculation here and Miss Parr would lunge.

As a matter of fact, she did lunge, but it was too late as Sam was able to slam the door shut and turned the key still placed in the lock. She was finally in control for the first time since arriving.

As she ran down the corridor towards the staircase by the kitchen, she could hear Miss Parr howling and banging against the door, still sounding like a monster.

She turned right and ran down the stairs towards the front door of the house, wasting no time in pushing them open, she stopped and recalculated her move, turned back and looked at the many candles now slowly running out of wax to burn through. She kicked a small table as she rushed, and candles fell to the floor. They were still lit as she left the house.

The night air was cold, her breath was visible as it drifted off in front of her before vanishing. The sea air helped her breathe while running a distance she wasn't used to.

She looked back over her shoulder to see flames licking the rooftops of the mansion house, flames devoured almost every window. She noticed lights in some of the houses nearby switching on. She wasn't sure who to trust in the town, but she remembered the old man sat outside his house and he seemed pleasant enough.

He lived in a small bungalow that had a steep concrete

pathway leading up to his door, there was a railing there to assist him considering his age it made sense. Sam used this to propeller herself to the front door and she banged on the frosted glass of No. 32 Whittingham Road. Lights erupted from beyond the glass, a blurry figure appeared slowly and the door opened a hand's width, a small figure of a man peeked through.
"Who is it?"
He seemed to be in a white vest top and boxer shorts, clearly he had just got out of bed. In fact Sam hadn't realised it was nearly three thirty in the morning.
"I need help, there are horrible people trying to kill me"
Sam was crying and patting on the door. She had realised at some stage she had dropped the glass shard on her escape, but she was still clutching at the bloodied fabric that was wrapping it.
The man slammed the door in her face and turned the light out, after all it was Halloween and it could have easily just been a prank.
"Hello?...Sir?"
Sam, hunched over, nearly fell over the concrete slab and slammed her hand on the glass, leaving a bloody handprint, as the curtains were shut and gave no indication of light beyond them.
Sirens wailed as Fire engines roared past on the road towards the house, she could smell the fire still from where she was standing, but the night was too black itself to see any smoke rising. She could see an orange glow on the horizon though.

A few moments pass, Sam is still standing on the same spot, looking in all directions, not quite sure what to do next.
The sirens of the ambulance and police could be heard now, and they must have come from a nearby town to assist. They hadn't come from the direction of town itself. Haunting the air with a ghostly echo and coloured lights reflected off the buildings that obstructed the view.
She headed further towards town, maybe she could find an old phone booth, she had never used one before and didn't have any change, she had never even noticed if they still existed.
As she turned a corner she bumped in a man with a big beard and long shaggy hair. He smiled at Sam with rotten yellow and black teeth and reached out at her, she dodged him and ran further down the path.

He was following her.

She reached the corner of the pavement as a car skidded in front of her, Richard, the policeman that drugged her dived out of the driver's seat towards her. She raced down the hill, being pursued by both men, then another two or three figures joined in the chase, then another five.
Reaching the high street, she didn't have a moment to spare on where to run and so she didn't think about that, she just kept running and noticed a man had leapt out of an alleyway in front of her. She quickly stopped, tried to anticipate his moves but then decided to run across the road to the other side of the street.

She ran through the old archway with victorian paintings either side, she found a couple of large green bins and tucked her way to the back in between them. It was a tight fit but also had a strong odour of fish.

She heard the footsteps in quick succession behind, some of them carried on past on the street while just a few sets had spun off towards where she was hiding, they came to a sudden halt.

"She's bloody vanished" the voice said, Perhaps with a Yorkshire accent. But he was clearly out of breath.

"I reckon she's still down the high street somewhere. Cmon" said the other voice, slightly younger and unrecognisable.

They both quickly disappeared back the other way and there was now silence.

Even though the stench of Fish was penetrating her nostrils, she wasn't moving yet. She took her time to breath and re-assess the situation in her mind.

30

As the house sat burning, there were at least twenty firemen with several hoses pointed at the base of the flames through the first floor window, another several of them had gone inside.
Florence stood watching the house burn. She was being patched up, sat on the back of the ambulance. Artemis sitting on the wall, the flames were reflecting in his eyes. Miss Parr felt lucky that Artemis had survived the flames. But she wasn't finished with Sam, she wanted her dead now.

no more games.

She pushed herself off the ambulance floor, where she was sitting with her feet dangling and picked up Artemis from the wall, holding him close to her chest and stroking the top of his head.
"Maam, you need to come back with us, you've inhaled a lot of smoke and need to be looked at further" Said the ambulance driver, shouting over the roaring flames he was a thin Indian man with thick rimmed glasses and wearing dark green scrubs. The other was a female with red hair and freckles, she was sitting filling in paperwork on the passenger seat.
Florence handed Artemis over to the policeman from out of

town and she headed off down the road towards the high street, she was walking with little emotion or speed, and she vanished from sight, like a ghost ship into the night.

31

The night sky was slowly becoming a shade lighter, birds had already begun to break into song. There was a shift in the wind, causing louder waves to crash into the rocks on the front.

In a deep sleep, the shops were still shuttered and the pubs had long since called time. Sam slipped through the maze of alleyways and backstreets, her steps hushed, her breath tight in her throat. It would become incredibly more difficult to avoid trouble with the sky becoming lighter.

Taking an unfamiliar turn, she found herself on the harbour which was an area she hadn't seen before. It was picturesque. The pier nestled around a small sandy beach cove. Aside it nestled into a cliffside were an assortment of small shops, one of them had fudge of every flavour imaginable displayed in the window and Sam found herself salivating. It had been a long while since she last ate, but she admitted to herself that she wouldn't be eating for some time yet.

Where the row of shops ended sat a few other buildings, there was the lifeboat station, an aquarium that looked pathetically small and a small boarded up building that looked like it housed a small pub at one time.

There was a tall statue further down, looking out to sea. It was a large steel sculpture of a pregnant female warrior, the insides of her pregnant stomach visible in a horrifically gory detail and she held a sword to the sky.

It was the most bizarre statue she had laid her eyes upon. The waves crashed beyond the brick wall, just beyond its gaze and in the distance through thin fog and ocean spray, sat a very large hillside. It seemed to be shaped like an elephant, lying on its belly.

Gulls swarmed in great circles around the harbour, occasionally diving at the water for fish. Bells were sounding from the tightly docked fishing boats and yachts that were anchored.

Sam was cold, there was a real chill in the air that morning and Sam wasn't dressed for the weather, she had a t- shirt that was stained with blood and an exposed stomach from ripping the shirt earlier that evening.

There was a small building at the top of a hill that overlooked the harbour, it was a lighthouse but the smallest she had ever seen, she slowly worked her way towards it, using the sharp slate wall that led up the hill.

Upon reaching the top, she noticed the black plume of smoke rising from the distance over the town, and realized it was the fire from the mansion house, it was now visible as the sky grew lighter.

A fisherman had now arrived in the harbour and was setting up on the wall by the statue, Sam was now deciding if she should approach him, he could be one of them.

32

Florence regrouped with Richard and some other townsfolk that were out looking for Sam. They gathered on the steps of the church in town.

"Any sign of her?" Richard was the first to speak as he lit a cigarette.

"No, but she couldn't have gone very far" Florence was holding her shoulder and then pulled over a black netted shawl to hide her injuries.

"Let me have a look" said a voice, a man stepped towards Florence, a bald man with thin rimmed glasses and was very scrawny. It was Dr Plemiton, he had been the doctor to most in Ilfracombe since the late seventies.

The doctor examined her wounds, but wasn't too concerned about them. "You'll be OK, just watch out for signs of infection" the man opened his leather bag and revealed some herbs, he pressed them against her wounds.

"Keep pressure on it for a while," he smiled.

The doctor, known for his unusual practices in medicine. Little did they know that he was struck off from medical school for these odd practices. But nobody in the town would ever question him, there was too much trust, and it was a different time back then.

Richard agreed to search the Harbour, while Miss Parr searched the gardens and Museum area on the front.

33

"Hello"
Sam had approached the fisherman, he was wearing a big green raincoat and wellies, his hood was up which concealed most of his head, only his face was visible which was wrinkled and aged, but certainly not older than fifty five.
"My god girl, are you OK?"
 The man dropped his fishing rod down and held her shoulders as it began to lightly rain, there was a soft patter of raindrops hitting the concrete around them, which was only drowned out by the waves that seemed to have increased in size and force.
"Please get me out of here, I need to leave… I…"
Sam was sobbing, the man pulled her in and hugged her, he was a stranger but she felt for the first time in days, some comfort, safety. She reminded the man of his daughter who he rarely had access to see.
"Come with me - i'll keep you safe" he grabbed his bait box and rod, shoved them back of his jeep and opened the passenger door for her. She hesitated for a second but the inside of the jeep was pristine and she had a wave of lemon hit her nostrils from the air fresher dangling from the rear view mirror.
"It's Ok, you can trust me" his promises seemed genuine. Sam climbed into the jeep, as she shut the door, the rain

seemed to come down heavier, obscuring the view until he turned the ignition and turned on the wipers.

"We'll go to my place, it's just on the outskirts of town, is someone after you?.. Yeah must be.. Look at you, you're terrified, and that blood, are you hurt?" The man was concerned.

"Graham, my name is Graham" he smiled and put his hand lightly on his shoulder for a split second, and retrieved it quickly worrying that he had made her feel uneasy. "Sam"

"Well, pleasure to meet you, I am sorry for whatever you've gone through Sam"

The Jeep pulled away and they headed out of the harbour, Sam gave a quick intake of breath with sheer panic as she saw Richard on foot, walking around the corner.

She ducked her head down, he didn't see her.

"Richard? Why is he after you?...He's… What did YOU do?" Graham halted the car with a high pitched whine of the brakes and Richard turned around and observed the Jeep that had suddenly halted.

"Please Graham, it's not like that he is bad, he wants to kill me, please"

Sam was in pure distress and Graham could see that. It looked genuine, but Graham was a psychologist either, but he also didn't want any trouble with police.

Without warning, he covered her with a blanket and winded down the window.

"Hello" Graham smiled at Richard, one thing he was good at was acting, thankfully.

"Spot of fishing? Leaving already?" Richard was soaking wet, he took the cigarette out of his mouth and looked at it, realizing it was too damp to smoke and he put it in his top jacket pocket.

"Yes of course but, the rain ya' know" Graham pointed up and smiled.

There was a pause as Richard looked in the back of the Jeep for a second, he stopped and just stared at Graham for a moment.

"I thought you fisherman loved the rain, good chance to catch?" he said, stepping closer to the window.

"Nah not me, my days of fishing in this kinda weather are past me!"

"Is that so?" Richard looked past him to something concealed under a blanket next to him on the passenger seat.

"I'm looking for a girl, have you seen one around here Graham?" Richard's eyes didn't leave the passenger seat.

"No No... I..."

Graham stopped and looked at the blanket, then back at Richard, then at the blanket. He slammed his foot on the accelerator as the Jeep jolted forward. Richard was hanging on.

"Stop you motherf..." Richard let go, he couldn't hold on any longer and Graham sped off, he could see Richard using his radio in the rear view as he became smaller and smaller.

Sam pushed the blanket off herself and turned to look behind and out the back window.

"Thank you"

"Don't thank me yet, we're going to be in the shit now, I don't know why he is after you but.. You can be damn sure we're gonna be wanted criminals" Graham shook his head, continuously checking his mirrors, expecting a trail of police cars to materialise.

"We can't go to my place now, we'll go to Willies, my brothers place"

Sam explained the whole story to Graham, from her arriving from an orphanage to Miss Parr and the boy's murder. She left out the ghosts though, that would probably be a bit too far.

"I thought you were crazy, but.. Ya know, a lot of these things add up" he scratched his head, continuing to over check his mirrors. They were driving country roads now as they drove out of the town, past the sign that Sam saw at the beginning of the week.

"Things in the town got weird in recent months, damn kids going missing, one was kinda normal right? Then two were worrying.. Then three.. Four… five.. A small town like this? Nah.." He shook his head again in disbelief.

"But you know what, I saw something like it on Netflix, not long ago actually, a cult in America. But in Ilfracombe? Who would have thought it"

There was no sign of life on the drive through backroads, they passed an old farm house or two, but no sign of life out there.

"Me and Willie were orphans too ya know, never knew my mother, heard my father was a drunk and a beater of women though"

The wind was causing the car to veer off slightly every now and then, they drove through huge potholes in the road that were unavoidable, but the jeep could handle it.

"The weather's getting wild, it wasn't forecast, that's why I decided to go fishing, I certainly picked a day for it" he chuckled to himself.

Sam stayed quiet, she was not only shy but worried about being followed, she hadn't seen any cars behind them at all. But she knew that she wasn't out of the woods just yet.

"This ol road still gives me the spooks you know, nineteen eighty three it was, a morning like this too. I was coming back from Sandy's.." he stopped and looked at Sam, smiled. "My first flame" he laughed to himself again and checked his mirrors once more.

"Yeah, comin back from Sandy's and I was coming to this bend here, something came out of the tree line, a white mist but it was walking like a person.. Sounds daft I know.. Ghost stories right?"

Sam's ears turned as she was now looking at him with curiosity.

"Yeah it stopped in the middle of the road, and looked at me and it shrieked as i slammed the brakes, but it was gone, i think i... drove right through it"

"I believe you" Sam put her hand on his arm with encouragement that was cradling the gearstick, before returning it to her lap.

"There were things happening in that house around me," she

continued.

They reached another small village, coming down a steep hill was a caravan site on the left and then shortly another on the right. They drove past a beach and some houses. "Longest village in Europe this one" Graham stuck a toothpick in his mouth.
The village stretched endlessly, it was all in the same the whole way through, houses on either side just sandwiched together, but nestled in a valley of houses that seemed to be very modern and must have belonged to rich and famous people as they were gated.
The Jeep parked up horizontally against the pavement, they both got out of the jeep and Graham guided her up a few concrete steps to a red front door.
He pushed the doorbell and then waited for an answer.

34

By morning, the house was still standing amongst smoke that had now turned white. The roof had mostly remained in place but had collapsed above the reception and main front doors, which had left a heap of slate tiles scattered across the gravel car park.
All of the windows in the house had broken due to the immense heat produced from the evening flames.
One of the elder firemen (amongst the three ladders from out of town still working on small fires) took off his hardhat and yellow fireproof gloves, he mopped the sweat and soot that had accumulated over the last seven hours on his brow. He took his bottle of water and poured it over his head, a refreshing feeling instantly came over him.
"Son of a bitch, this house is going to survive again" he muttered to another man next to him, now copying exactly what he had just done.
"Again?"
The younger man was observing the water gauge now on the truck.
"This house has seen fire after fire, most of the buildings in town have been taken down by just one, my first fire was at this place back in the sixties, a whole bunch of kids perished, it was awful" the man was now placing his hardhat and gloves back on. "We need to do another sweep inside, we'll take one

of the windows, there is no getting through the front now, the roof is completely blocking the entrance now" the man threw his finger in different directions, signalling the men around him to take on new tasks.

His eye was caught by something he had just seen in one of the top windows, a figure. He was initially about to shout to his men that there was someone inside but he had lost all train of thought, he had completely zoned out from the situation now as two piercing eyes were staring into his soul. It was a small child, there were no real facial features, just dark and burnt skin from head to toe, there were flakes of loose flesh waving in the breeze all over the chest and legs.

When he finally came to and back into the moment, the figure had vanished. He quickly glanced over all the windows surrounding, but nothing.

35

"Graham? I wasn't expecting- who's this?"
A hunched over unkept man had answered the door, he had a long matted beard and long brown hair that was sticking up in all different directions. He was wearing a dark blue t-shirt that had seemingly never been washed and wore joggers that seemed to be held together by the stains.
"Sorry, i'll explain Willie"
They huddled through the front door and into the small open plan flat, it was dark, the curtains were closed and the room was smokey, Sam found the smell of the place not so pleasant. There were dead plants all over the place and piles of DVD's that had some rather disturbingly positioned naked women all over the covers.
Sam's only option to sit down was on a stained corduroy sofa that was covered in newspaper and tissues. A large black and white XL bulldog stumbled into the room, looking like he was struggling to walk with the weight of his own muscle. He sat in the corner by the TV and started to scratch himself with an insane glint in his eye. "Willis!" Willie smiled, but the dog continued to scratch.
Graham never mentioned anything about the state of the flat, or the x rated DVD's or even the tissue that he had just flicked off the sofa. Sam guessed this was standard for this Willie

character.

"This is Sam, she asked for my help - there is something strange happening in Ilfracombe Willie"

Willie had brought over a can of Red Stripe and placed it down on the glass coffee table in front of him, he had placed a second in front of Sam and smiled.

"She's a bit young for that, and it's a bit early for me" Graham swiped the second can in front of Sam and pushed them both towards the other side of the table towards Willie, who had already cracked open a can himself with a small hiss.

"Suit yerself"

Graham continued to tell the entire story to Willie, occasionally Sam would correct him on some mistakes for her side of it, but mostly she kept quiet and watched Willie's expressive reaction. Graham made a point to re-iterate that Richard (they referred to him as the sheriff, like a small American town in Maine) had tried to get to Sam through Graham, and was most likely on a manhunt for him too.

"Blimey"

Willie sat back as Willis led across his lap, occasionally fidgeting and giving out a sigh, as though we were disturbing his peace.

"I have a buddy in Ilfracombe, Simon, perhaps I'll give him a call" Willie scratched his head as he scanned the room with his eyes, wondering where he put his phone. Another XL Bully had stumbled into the room, it was drooling across the carpet with its eyes on Graham, giving the look of seeing an old friend.

"Hey Bruce!" Graham stroked the all black all muscle hound vigorously, in which he was delighted and his tail wagged left to right in quick succession.
"Can you trust this Simon?"
Graham grasped his knee anxiously, thinking about all of the people he knew in Ilfracombe that were associated with Richard.
"Sure I can, we've known each other since the ol' sea cadet days"
He smiled as he realised his phone was in his pocket all along. Punching in a few buttons on the brick of a phone, each with a musical tone. Willie placed the phone to his ear.

36

Richard was creeping through the residential streets of Ilfracombe in his car. The window was rolled down as he slowly lurched around corners, he was not only using his sight but listening for noise as well. He wasn't prepared to let them escape his grasp. He would stop at the curb occasionally to ask locals if they had seen Graham or Sam but to no advantage.
 Several hours had passed and he was starting to lose hope in finding them. He pulled up on the side of the road that looked over at Hele Bay, a small connected area to Ilfracombe that had over the years been considered its own separated town. It sat in a valley between two rolling cliffs and had more pubs than houses or shops.
Richard rolled up and smoked the finest mary jane you could source in a hundred square miles. It cleared his mind and sharpened his senses (or his paranoia) he took a call from Miss Parr, who was on the other side of Ilfracombe and was also coming to a dead end with the search.
"Call yerself an honest, justice-serving policeman huh?" a familiar voice from the back seat of the car.
Not again, fuck please no.
Richard adjusted the rear view mirror to see the backseat of the car and a familiar man sat there staring at him with blood shot eyes, his skin was a dark grey with a hint of green, his cheek bones protruding through the leathery dead skin, a hole

in his cheek exposed his rotten teeth and dark gums. It was Micky.

"You're fucking dead, i am not going to sit here and talk to a corpse!"

Richard took the last drag of his spliff and threw it out the window.

"I can't wait for you to experience the pain i felt, death is nothing but fuckin' pain Rich, and its coming for you"

Micky was now laughing as flies began to dart around the backseat and then into his mouth.

Richard screamed in terror and pulled at his hair, hoping the figure of his ex boss would disappear but it just continued to laugh at him.

"She did something to my mind Mick, she made me push you"

Tears rolled down his distraught face, he was always showing himself to be tough as nails in front of anyone. But right now something inside him had snapped.

"Do the right thing and just kill yourself"

Micky was gone, Richard had stopped crying, his breath was shallow and difficult to get back under his control. His head was thumping with pain and his vision blurred.

37

"Simon is really into all that occult and witchy stuff. I bet he already knows what the fuck is going on over -"
He was interrupted when Simon finally answered the phone.
"Simon, how ya doing bud?"
Both Bruce and Willis looked up at their owner with intrigue, realised they were not being spoken to and then went back to sleep, both of their heads on Graham's lap and fighting for the most attention.
Sam could hear a faint voice on the other line from where she was sitting, but her attention was too drawn to the sound of cars outside, she fully expected Miss Parr to burst in at any moment.
Simon explained what was happening, and no surprise to Willie that Simon had been following this cult for a while and he was struggling to find out their intentions.
"Ok, see ya soon"
Willie hung up the phone and looked at Graham with a hopeful nod.
"This guy knows his shit, he might be able to help"
Willie began to roll a cigarette.
"Help with what? What are we going to do, go in there like Clint Eastwood and take on the town?" Graham laughed

sarcastically.

"That's… not a bad idea"

Willie laughed, but Graham wasn't having fun at all.

"So, Sam wasn't it? Why you an orphan then?"

Willie licked the paper of his cigarette, rolled it and placed it behind his ear, then began to roll another.

"I don't think Sam would want to talk about that Willie"

Graham felt awkward at this moment, he paused and looked at Sam.

"It's OK, I never knew my parents, there is no dramatic story there, spent the first six years of my life in an orphanage before going to foster carers, it was nice for a long while until it wasn't"

Sam's expressionless face quickly frowned thinking about Mr Forester's wandering hands.

"Well me and Graham here, both dint know our parents neither"

Willie dragged on his cigarette while Graham said nothing, he was now just observing the dogs on his lap as they both were drooling excessively.

"So.. what do you do?"

Sam asked, her hands on her lap and she was edging off the sofa, she didn't like the thought of what she was sitting on.

Willie gave a cheeky smile, his teeth were in pretty good shape compared to the rest of him and his flat too.

"Well, not something we should discuss at your age-"

"He's a..director" Graham smiled

Sam put two and two together and felt horrified in his

presence now.

"You see there's good evil, and there is bad evil i guess" Willie laughed as his cigarette had gone out, he relit it.

"No it's all pretty much bad evil" Graham muttered under his breath, but Willie ignored it.

They continued to lightly talk, mostly Graham and Willie as they debated if Ryan next door was gay, Ruth across the street was part of this cult or if the Indian guy who ran the corner shop was a murderer on the run from his home country. This went on for another thirty to forty five minutes and then the doorbell went.

Willie jumped to his feet, the dogs sprung to life and followed him. He pulled the latch down and opened the door.

"Come in bud!" Willie guided a man through the door.

He ducked under the doorframe, and there stood a man at a height that Sam had never seen, he must have been six foot seven inches at the least. The man had sandy blonde long hair and was very lanky, he wore a black baggy t-shirt that said Ron Jon, Cocoa Beach FL and had baggy cut off trousers and checkered trainers.

"Killer swell out there Will" he bumped fists with Willie, he offered to Graham but he just looked lost in this dialect and just put his thumb up. Simon looked at Sam and just said "Aight" and nodded.

38

THE DAY BEFORE

Waves rolled beneath the board, they were working together it seemed, in absolute harmony. The water was cold but it didn't bother Simon at all. He was in his element at this moment and had complete control, it's like the board wasn't even there and he was breaking waves with his feet in his mind. The cold water splashed against his shins and he loved that feeling. The swell was quick to build that morning but had calmed as quick as they rose.
Simon shook his head as he strolled out of the shallow waters with his board under his arm. He shook his head like a dog would, and sprayed out in all directions. He gazed across the deserted beach, in the distance he could see other Surfers walking back in, it looked kinda creepy to him, like ghosts walking out of the tide in thin fog.
 Sand beneath his feet and between his toes parted away as he walked further away from the water, the sand became warmer and dryer the further he got, avoiding the occasional jellyfish, seaweed and debris that had washed up.
In the distance he saw a beautiful sight, a girl, around his age as well. It was the middle of summer and she was wearing a

onesie that hugged her well and was showing off her curves. She was wearing a large straw sun hat, underneath he could see her bright blonde hair, she was sitting on the wall looking out to sea, her arms spread out and were resting back on the wall.

"Hey" Simon smiled, he was considered a heart throb by most girls his age, and older too, much to his surprise when he knocked on his neighbours door once to find her half naked sixty year old body in front of him.

"Hey yourself" the girl said and smiled.

"Not a surfer?" Simon's best ice breaker.

"Not particularly, tried it once and wasn't very good" she looked at the palm of her hands, indented with the pattern of the wall as she brushed off some of the grit.

"Ah it's kinda easy once you get the hang of it, just need the right waves ya know" he smiled again and quickly followed up "Names Simon" he offered to shake her hand like a gentleman and she accepted. "Claire"

She pushed herself off the wall and brushed off her backside, Simon was looking but didn't want her to catch him this early on in the game.

"Fancy a drink?" They were walking side by side aimlessly for a moment, but already unconsciously headed in the direction of the woolacombe beach front bar.

"Sure" Claire said, tucking her hair behind her ear, this made Simon smile, he knew the signs that a girl liked him. It was like clockwork to him, he smiles and acts like a gent and she will play with her hair.

"So you live nearby?" Simon asked, they were sitting at the bar and drinking summery cocktails, he was drinking a pina colada and she ordered sex on the beach. Simon felt excited when she had ordered this and to him felt like he was on a winner. Simon sucked through the straw and tasted the sweet, creamy, and refreshing blend of pineapple, coconut, and rum.
"Ilfracombe, actually. You?" she smiled as she also tasted her fruity cocktail topped with a ton of ice.
"No way! Me too, how have we never met?" he laughed, this was exciting, all the girls in Ilfracombe were either 'been there done that, worn the t-shirt' or a big no-no.
"Well my Brother Richard you might know, he works for the police?" she continued to slurp on the drink, which was disappearing fast and so he signalled the barman for another.
"Yeah of course, Richard! He might have… arrested me a couple of times" he presented a half frown, but was playing it cool and much to his amusement she was laughing.
"He would literally arrest someone for breathing I swear, what are you a drug dealer or something?" she said sarcastically.
Fuck that was on the nose and correct, well part time at least. Simon just laughed in response and sipped from his drink, quickly thinking to change the subject.
"So why are you out here alone?" He questioned, it did seem strange for a girl on her own, on a big beach and not surfing.
"I come out here a lot by myself, my family are ….intense sometimes" she said with a sad tone as she looked out towards the sea again.
They continued to talk, they exchanged hobbies, she spoke

about her love for film and how she wanted to be a writer. He expressed his love for seventies movies like Jaws and she admitted she'd never seen it. He would jokingly mock her and it made her laugh more.

"Hey, can I get your number?" he asked her, she nodded and smiled and punched it into his phone. More tourists from the hotels nearby started pouring onto the beach and the bar slowly became more crowded too. They both took this as a sign to leave and they parted ways with a wave.

Simon started the drive back to Ilfracombe with a smile, at first it was just a natural attraction to Claire, but as they continued to talk he felt a real connection. He hadn't felt that for a long time. He jabbed at a button on the CD player and blasted Nice To Know You by Incubus. He sang along at the top of his voice (albeit slightly out of tune) as the Nissan X Trail picked up speed along the winding country roads. This journey was quite solitary, there were just a few cars that passed him on the way back through and it was never flat terrain, it was endless winding roads through tree topped valleys, often coming to single track roads where you would have to honk your horn around sharp corners.

The afternoon hit mid point, the sun was beating through the windscreen onto Simon's already tanned arms. He had made his way through all his favourite surf rock tunes including his favourite bands greatest hits The Red Hot Chili Peppers.

Before he knew it, there was the dreaded sign welcoming him to Ilfracombe.

Welcome back to the shithole

He drove through Hele Bay and up through Hillsborough, or the sleeping elephant as people called it. Simon thought it was dumb, a hill called Hillsborough, so creative. But it was once an Iron age fort and now a nature reserve of sorts.
Then past the local leisure centre, where he worked as a life guard on weekends.
It wasn't so bad in the summer when tourists would stop by. You would occasionally get the good lookers, but it was dreadful when the winter came and all the old biddies with their sagging breasts slapped against the water.
Good ol Brenda and her water zumba class which with one small thought made Simon shiver as he instinctively turned up Primus on his stereo.
As he drove into a quiet cul-de-sac, he was home.
Although hopefully not for much longer here, he still lived with his parents, his father was a fisherman and the catch had been very poor in recent months. He blamed it on the warmer climate bringing larger predators to the shores. His mother was a piano teacher and her business was actually pretty successful. She claimed to have taught Elton John as a boy, but Simon knew it was probably Elton Johns, the guy who ended up in a padded cell because he would chase kids down the street and bark at them like a dog on all fours.
Parking up the family sized car (which he only bought to fit his board in) Simon left the board in the back, he'd grab it later and wax it down probably. He walked through the front door and past his mother in the spare room, she was in the middle of a class, you could tell as some kid was playing

chopsticks badly.

Into the kitchen, where his dad was watching the rugby on his new ipad, that he struggled to operate, he was shouting as he had his earphones in and didn't realise how loud he was being. Simon grabbed an apple from the bowl and turned back towards the stairs up to his room, taking a bite out of the juicy red sphere, it oozed with flavour in his mouth and between his teeth.

His bedroom was dimly lit, and very messy, he had clothes sprawled out all over his bed, the floor, on the desk chair in front of his computer that was left on constantly and giving a constant rattle and hum. And the room smelt of last night's Pizza, which was still on the desk baking in the sunlight that beamed through the gap in the curtains. He had surf related posters on the wall, mostly bikini clad women on boards in some tropical paradise, but he also had bands he liked on the wall too. It mostly covered the entire wallspace but often revealed hints of the old Victorian wallpaper behind it.

He switched on his TV, which was an old style CRT one, he had illegally hooked up the downstairs sky box to mirror it onto his, so he was at the mercy of what his parents had on in the evenings which was mostly soaps. But right now it was still on Kerrang! from his last watch.

He dropped onto his back on the springy single bed, he bit into the remainder of his apple and then flung it across the room onto the pizza box without a thought of cleanliness. Taking out his phone, he hovered over Claire's number. *Too early to text her? Is that uncool? Shit I don't know.* He hesitated, started to type a text, and then stopped and dropped his phone beside him. He was now staring at the ceiling indecisively.

39

Claire sat on the steps outside her house, she could hear her family shouting at each other. Richard stormed out moments later in his uniform and disappeared up the road.
Recently, a woman from the big house up the road had stopped by and presented gifts. She was new in the town and wanted to make a good impression on people and Claire's family were quite influential around town. Nothing would have been out of the ordinary if since she started visiting, weird things hadn't started to happen.
First the dog, Dobby (after the house elf of course) had suddenly spontaneously combusted on the living room rug. It became a famous event, the papers had been at the door from all over.
Then Dad's lovebirds, they fought to the death and both died. And most recently, Dad put himself in the hospital as he had electrocuted himself. He was certain he turned the mains off, but in fact the entire house was still live when he was wiring in the new oven.
It all started when she came by and blessed the house with some strange ritual she had claimed came from her heritage. Richard had suddenly become good friends with Miss Parr and it didn't make much sense. Then Micky died and he got his promotion and it all began to slip into place like a jigsaw

puzzle. She hated to think that Richard had something to do with his death but he had changed over the last weeks. First he would just not be at home even outside of work hours, he would come smelling strange and would bring home herbal remedies for their mother's poor back. But then he would start bringing trinkets home and he would be obsessed with dark stories, ghosts and demons.

Now they all just argued, sometimes it would just happen for no reason and spiral out of control like this moment.

Claire was grasping her phone, hoping that she would receive a text from Simon, she was quite mesmerized by him that morning. He seemed care free or free spirited. He didn't seem trapped in a cage like her, she was being asked to come along to a party that night at the big house. She had a horrific feeling about the whole thing.

40

The night was dark, an owl hooted in the distance as Simon was strumming along to Chili Peppers on his fender strat guitar in the dark. Dreaming of being on a big stage, spotting Claire in the crowd and showing off during a guitar solo (which he couldn't actually play all that well)
The phone, set on vibrate, pulsated through the mattress beside him as it lit up the wall. In a rush of adrenaline he grabbed it with excitement, and now felt nervous seeing Claire's name pop up on the screen. He hesitated to answer, but he did of course.
"Well hey-"
He was interrupted by sobbing
"I didn't know who else to call.. She killed him" Claire wasn't making any sense to him, and was just sobbing and trying to breathe through her blocked nose. She sounded distraught.
"What's going on?"
Simon was stunned, not just by this moment and what she meant but the fact that she was trusting him already.
Claire over the period of the next twenty minutes, told the story to Simon, consisting of their family heading up to the mansion house. They were greeted and had a lovely dinner but the place was spooky and the guests mostly seemed to be acting odd, and some of the townspeople she knew were not like themselves.

She had drunk some wine, and the next thing she knew she was in a church wearing matching robes with everybody else, chanting and howling like crazy, her head was burning and her eyes distorted. She saw Miss Parr slit a boy's throat and had sipped from his blood. The worst part was that it was not forced, she took it and didn't fight it.

Before long, Claire apologised and didn't want to drag him into something so wicked and swore that she would get help. That was the last Simon ever heard from her, she stopped answering his calls and messages.

41

PRESENT DAY

Simon sat back in the arm chair in the corner of the room in amazement. "So, why did you call me?" he was then scratching his head in confusion.
"Well you know about this stuff right?" Willie encouraged him to be more open on the subject.
"Will - man, I did a project in Year 8 on Wicca, that's literally it" he laughed in amazement at how much Willie had made him sound like some kind of expert demonologist and continued "Wicca is like the good one, white magic and that. This is something else" Simon looked to the floor and swallowed hard, remembering Claire and that he hadn't heard from her.
"Willie.." Graham was disappointed.
"We are wasting time" Graham was frustrated now and shrugged off the dogs from his lap and stood up with his hands on his hips and his head bearing down with all of its sudden weight.
"Whatever you guys do, I am in.. i need to find Claire" Simon said eagerly while everyone suddenly wondered the same question. Who's Claire? Instantly Simon became telepathic but then realised he hadn't explained.
"I met her on the beach, we got talking, she's Richard's sister

and she is in some kind of trouble, spoke about how someone killed someone else" Simon was up and pacing the small room.

"What about the police outside of the area? - reach out to another authority?" Sam questioned them, but she felt like it was a dumb one until she was acknowledged by Graham.

"That might be our only option, but we just have to hope that this doesn't stretch out further" Graham was concerned and clearly anxious.

"It's ilfracombe, were in the ass end of the world and its always been full of fuckin whacko's" Simon was nodding in agreement.

Simon pulled out his phone and tapped away.

"We can call Barnstaple station?"

"No, it's too close, I was thinking maybe Exeter" Graham was visualising the map of Devon in his mind.

Simon punched in the number for Exeter and it began to ring, he put it on loud speaker and placed it on the coffee table in the middle of everyone.

"I'll do the talking" Graham said, he was always one to take lead in situations.

A man's voice answered, and Graham kept calm and explained the story - he was halfway through when the voice interrupted him amongst the background noise of other telephones.

"Sir, is this a joke?"

"No, it's -"

He was interrupted again.

"If this is a case within the jurisdiction of North Devon, i'll patch you through there"
"No you fuckin tool -" Willie interrupted, he was also now on his feet. But it was too late, and the phone line was ringing again, this time it was Trisha from the Ilfracombe station. Simon hung up immediately.
"Great now they are gonna trace it, were fucked!" Willie panicked.
Graham just laughed in disbelief at Willie, not only did he think they were in the middle of some american manhunt and that Ilfracombe somehow had this know-how to do that, but also how much drugs was he on?
"I highly doubt that Trisha Rivers has the capability to trace that call" Simon joked, scratching his head again with nerves.
"Look I'll go to my car and speak with Exeter again" Graham walked out and Willie followed.
Simon nervously looked at Sam, didn't know what to say, hated the awkward silence. "I'll just err-" he pointed out the door and then followed the others.
Sam sat down and observed her wounds, they were still hurting and she was covered in deep scratches from being dragged. Her jaw was in agony from the slap she took from Miss Parr.
Sam led back on the sofa, she ignored the mess now, she was too tired to deal with anything else, she closed her eyes and focused on steadying her breathing, she slowly drifted to sleep.
Memories drifted into her consciousness, she knew she was

present but she didn't have any control over her movements. She was in the corridors of the orphanage again. The warm sunlight beating through the large windows and onto her face. But it was deserted. She couldn't hear the click clacking of the keyboards from the offices, she couldn't hear any children playing, and she couldn't even hear the clock ticking away on the wall. Moving down the hall she was not walking, she was floating and she felt it in her stomach, that feeling of a dip in the road. The door in front of her opened by itself with a slow and eerie precision. The atmosphere had shifted in an instant, the room went dark, cold and the smell of rotting flesh devoured her nostrils. Miss Parr's face appeared from the dark recesses beyond the door. Her face morphed, it was rotting in front of her, eyes bulged and leaked down her cheeks. Her tongue stretched out and dried out and was being pummeled by her teeth falling out of her receding gums. She made a horrific death rattle from the back of her throat and reached blindly for Sam.

She awoke with a blood curdling scream and with hazy and blurred vision, she was somewhere else now, it was dark and the seat was rumbling. She quickly realised she was in the back seat of Graham's car, but she couldn't move, her wrists and feet were tied with cables.

She screamed out, but realised she had a sock in her mouth and could taste what could only be described as Cheesy feet. "Fuck" putting his hands over his face, Willie was in the passenger seat. Simon was next to her in the backseat and they were going down a country road at some speed.

"I am sorry Sam" Graham was looking at her in the rear view mirror.
Simon cut in "Look, Richard said if we hand you over, we can just get on with our lives and Claire will be safe too"
Sam couldn't believe the selfish act, but at the same time it made some sense to her.
Would she have done the same thing?
They were now rolling past the welcome sign to town, it filled Sam with absolute dread, she felt a black cloud lingering over her, in the shape of the memory of Miss Parr.
Not from the signpost, Richard was leaning on his car waiting for them.
They pulled up beside him and Richard gave a creepy smile.
"Thank you boys, i'll take it from here" Richard pulled out a large spanner from his car and smashed it against Graham's skull, it split as blood sprayed onto the car window that Sam was watching from.
Willie screamed his brother's name in absolute terror before he was silenced too, another several blows to his skull as it turned to red mush onto the ground and became unrecognisable.
Simon had fled, he was running down the road at full speed. Richard was showing no care for him, he spat onto the ground and threw the spanner into the bushes beside the road.
Richard took the wheel of the car, he looked back at Sam and smiled again.
"Buckle up"
Richard was racing down the street at what seemed like sixty miles per hour, hitting Simon with such force he went straight

underneath the tyres and the car bounced violently, it sent Sam bouncing off her seat and half into the front of the car.
Richard screamed with adrenaline, like a possessed creature as his eyes were glowing orange. Sam turned to look out the back window, Simon was lying in the middle of the road covered in red, and the tires left a red trail along the road too.
"I'll get you back to her, then we are back on track, you're in some damn trouble but it's not my place, you belong to her"
Richard was laughing but also twitching, like he was coming off a high and needed another fix soon.
Richard took out his walkie from his vest pocket and pressed the side button which greeted with a static hiss.
"I've got the girl Florence, where shall we meet?"
There was silence for a moment but it was quickly broken.
"The lighthouse"
The car slowed to a regular speed, Richard certainly seemed to be coming down from it all as he jerked around in his seat.
"This isn't you" a male voice suddenly appeared in the passenger seat next to him, it was Micky's corpse again.
"Fuck off, not now" Richard spat the words, taking his sight from the road and glancing over to the passenger seat.
To Sam, there was nobody sitting there and no voices, she remained silent and observed Richard's crazy conversation with thin air.
"Stop it, your fuckin' dead" Richards jaw was clenched as he exposed his teeth, he was clearly losing his mind.
"Yeah we are dead" sat behind him was Willie's corpse, but his face was completely mangled and had an exposed brain

which was leaking down and onto the seat.

"Kill yourself and let her go" Micky grabbed the wheel and yanked it but Richard gained control of it and it tore off one of Micky's fingers and it landed somewhere on Richards lap, green liquid oozed from it and covered his trousers. It frightened Sam, still not seeing or hearing what he was witnessing, thinking she was about to be in a crash and that they were driving too close beside a thick stone wall.

Within seconds the car had clipped the wall and sent it into a spin, Richard's face crashed against the steering wheel with a loud cracking sound, which was the bone in his nose breaking. Sam was pushed into the front of the car and the cable around her ankles had snapped off, freeing her legs.

The door on her side was jammed against the wall, she would have to climb over Richard to get out, his face was against the wheel and he wasn't moving, smoke was pouring out of the bonnet of the car.

She pushed him back into his seat, he slumped and still didn't move, blood covered his nose which was twisted out of place. Sam could see his stomach rising and falling.

She slowly reached over towards the door handle, not taking her eyes off Richard and waiting for him to open his eyes and grab her. But he remained still, the walkie went off with a static hiss and it made Sam jump back into her seat, causing broken glass to shift around the interior of the car.

She slowly reached for the handle again, his nose twitched and she stopped for a second, but swallowed her anxieties and continued, she pulled at the handle and the car door was open slightly, she pushed it with her hands still tied, now the hard part though as she shifted herself over him, the most vulnerable position that he would have no doubt gotten some sexual kick from if he was conscious.

She was careful not to press the horn on the wheel and with that she was free and out of the car.

Her hands bound, she realised she was near the seafront and didn't know this area well. It was silent, the little life the town once had was gone completely and it was like a ghost town.

42

No matter which direction Sam walked, Miss Parr's presence lingered—like a shadow that didn't just follow her, but loomed above her.

A metallic taste coated the back of her throat. Warm, thick, and oppressive. It reminded her of the nosebleeds she used to get during summer—when heat and pollution stirred up her sinuses. Back then, it was just the weather. Now, it came with something far worse: a crawling dread that curled deep in her gut.

Then came a prickling sensation. It crept over her skin—not goosebumps, but something hungrier. It felt like the air itself was draining the strength from her limbs, making every step a quiet struggle.

Losing her footing, she used the palm of her hands to stay on her toes. The feeling of the concrete scraping her palms and with each forceful push she gave herself momentum.

   Early evening was setting in, thick and fluffy clouds began to bulge and stretch over the skies above. A golden sky was like a backlight to them, giving a deceiving heavenly glow that shone through trees and bounced off window panes.

   There was no one around, it was like everybody was locked in their homes and had to turn out the lights. Most of the curtains were drawn in the windows. It seemed that when Sam would step towards any light source it would fade away or suddenly extinguish.

She felt utterly alone, and brushing her mouth with the back of her arm she had now realised blood was running from the sides of her dry and cracked lips. Her glasses were filthy with smudges, grit and dried blood.

She stumbled past the sunspot arcade, it was shuttered and locked up with two big silver padlocks. There were fish and chip shops, gift shops and coffee houses that were all closed up.

Then past the foot of capstone, walking past a crazy golf course, it had windmills that were not spinning, there was no breeze, the waves were quiet as they smashed against the rocks nearby.

I need a moment.

Sam almost collapsed onto the wooden bench that was backed onto the foot of the hill and overlooked a church and its perfectly mowed front lawn.

A cold sweat had broken out all over her body, her eyes were blurred again and she was trembling. Not knowing if she was bleeding inside, exhaustion or a new collection of symptoms from her usual panic attacks.

She led on her side, stretching out on the bench. Feeling like she had let her guard down for a moment. She didn't care at this particular moment in time. Struggling to build the energy just to move her arms.

She felt like a battery that had been drained, and was

being pushed on its last ounce of power. Like a torch that is being used to the very last moment of death.

It seemed like an eternity before she was able to start moving again, she was able to swing her legs off the bench and was now in a sitting position. She looked out over the front, having an advantageous field of view. If someone was to appear, she would have plenty of warning and had her back only to the foot of the hill.

Now she was alone and it was quiet, her mind started edging towards the dark past. She thought about everything that had happened in her life all at once. A busy noise filled her mind, voices echoing not physically in her ears but they might as well have been.

You deserve this, you should just end it all.

Dark thoughts came like a wave, or like the warm up of an orchestra that led to the beginning of a loud crescendo.

She felt emotions, but she couldn't determine what they were. Guilt, Shame, Hate, Love, Sadness, Pity.. what were these things and how did you determine which one you are feeling?.
But also a numbness, and a floating sensation that mimics a subtle variation of vertigo symptoms.

I can't swallow, I can't breathe, I am going to choke.

That utter panic, as if you just swallowed a boiled sweet

whole, or a piece of gum you were told should never be swallowed or you'll choke and die.

The heart then begins to take centre stage, the main event. A thudding on the rib cage, like a creature trying to rip its way through the flesh.

Heart attack, i am dying, i need to move.

An impulse to move, it didn't matter where, it just had to happen. But the legs were jelly. Sam couldn't walk, she had to instantly sit down again after standing up. Normally she would retreat to a bathroom because she would be able to lock the door and secretly fight the feeling until it faded away.
Will it fade this time?
As quickly as it emerged, the symptoms eased and vanished into the fading day. All that was left now was the wreckage, the aftermath, the time to rebuild.
Bathing in her own sweat, tears and taste of blood, Sam rose to her feet. At this stage she would go to sleep, because she wouldn't have the energy to lift her eyelids. But this time was a surprise to her, she had a new burst of energy to survive as she found with her new strength, her bound wrists were free. Perhaps it was the realisation that a figure had emerged at the end of the street, slowly walking into focus. The figure was limping and clutching their side, they were definitely injured and it was definitely Richard.
"Found you" Richard was pale, a sheet of white, the only deep colour was blood that was smeared on his arms and face. But

he still found the internal power to laugh like someone who had completely lost themselves.

Sam found herself running again, she was surprising herself now as she was able to stand fairly tall and stable. Maybe not for long but at that moment she knew she could outrun him. She had come to a short junction of shops and restaurants, still with no sign of life but she could hear faint singing, it sounded like a church choir, but with a sinister agenda. It was the sound she had heard previously back at the house and the shape of the small junction was creating a slight breeze, like a wind tunnel and with that carried the singing louder and more distinct.

The sky was slowly taking a darker tone. There was no sun now, and the orange glow had gone..leaving a cold chill. Crossing the street she noticed a man, he was waving at her. Help?

As she stepped closer her heart sank, it was a mannequin that had a hydraulic moving arm. She would usually find it creepy but she had already witnessed worse things.

Looking back over her shoulder, Richard had turned the corner. He wasn't gaining on her but he wasn't giving up either.

Walking past an open metal gate, she peered through as she could hear old music playing. There was a man sitting at the far end of the alley with no emotion as he sat next to a gramophone. An old skinny man in Victorian clothing was just fixed in her direction, looking almost straight through her. He didn't move. The record was turning, slightly bobbing under the needle.

She leaned her back against a thorn
All alone and so lonely
And there she has had three babies born
All down by the greenwood sidey

The man suddenly stood up with the creak of his wooden rocking chair as it lifelessly continued to rock itself. The man smiled and started dancing, clapping and clicking his fingers on the spot.

She pulled a knife so long and sharp
All alone and so lonely
And pierced those babies innocent hearts
All down by the greenwood sidey.

The tall gate, with flaking green paint slammed shut in front of her. The music had instantly stopped, she could see nothing but blackness beyond its bars.
Richard had gained slightly on her and so she pressed forward and down the harbour, but she realised she was coming to a dead end, towards the lighthouse on the hill and where he wanted her to be.
It was either the hands of Miss Parr or the cruel chances of the sea.
Lights danced within the small house at the top of the hill, there was a small sign explaining its history and it was titled

'The Lantern House' voices in song bounced down the hillside and ricocheted off everything possible, with the turn of her head she would hear it slightly closer or further away.

The sky was moving to blackness now, drained of its colour under the rotating beam of light from the chapel roof.

An organ was playing underneath the layers of voices, there were higher feminine voices accompanied by the lowest baritone singing she had ever heard.

Richard was onto her shadow, his eyes wild and his smile widening.

"There is nowhere to go, you are meant to come with us, it's his wish, would you deny a god?"

He started to sound like a priest, or someone with an older tongue and definitely didn't seem like the same person.

However bad he was previously, he was now lost in his own mind.

She was slowly backing away, she continued to do so until she felt the cold metal railing behind her that was stopping her from stepping off the pier, end of the line.

"Can you hear them? The lost ones?"

She could hear something, amongst the waves.

The more she tuned to the tones, the less it sounded like crashing waves. It had morphed into groans, mass wailing of tortured souls. She turned towards the horizon of the dark green rippling sea. Peering down at where the waves broke against the support beams of the wooden pier, there was no water at all.

It was an endless sea of twisted grey rotting bodies, stumbling over each other, trying to climb the rotting wooden beams, falling over each other, naked but featureless, except for the face.

"Years of suffering will await you if you turn your back on him" Richard was dead panned now, all of his smile vanquished as it began to rain.

She turned back to the sea, it had returned to the dirty colour it was previously as water crashed against the beams below.

Richard grabbed her, pulling her arms behind her back into a position that he would most likely use on drunkards outside the pub on kick out time.

Sam struggled for a moment, but the more she did it would cause pain and so she stopped trying and felt defeated in an instant.

External white lights lit up the exterior of the small chapel on the hill, she felt that somehow the spirit of the mansion house had somehow imprinted on this place, she could feel an evil oozing from every nook and cranny.

Sounds of singing became louder, and the small size of the chapel became so evident on approach. It seemed to give a forced perspective, it seemed larger from the bottom of the hill or at the end of the harbour.

She reached the small doorway into the Chapel, the wooden door was damaged and cracked and hanging on one hinge, held open with a large rock.

The room inside was packed with hooded figures all facing Miss Parr, who had her arms raised up towards the ceiling, her gaze fixed upwards too.

The crowd opened up slightly, creating a small path for Sam. Richard shoved her into the center before vanishing amongst the hooded forest.

"Shall we begin?"

43

Candles flickering around them, Miss Parr's head bowed to Sam. She was visibly younger, more life behind the eyes and more evil perched on her lips.
"The night is young, and my child returns"
Sam felt a disgusting and wrenching feeling in her stomach, to be called her child was repulsive to her.
Hooded figures circled Sam, dropping their hands to the ground, shifting and then raising them, in a theatrical dance-like motion. They were singing and chanting.
The floor seemed to tremble in the small space beneath Sam's feet, The ground felt like it was shifting with the sheer amount of people in such a small space.
"I am not your child, and your home is nothing but ashes"
Sam spat in Miss Parr's direction as she said this.
To Sam's surprise, she just smiled.
"My girl, a house is a house, the real darkness is carried wherever you go, the spirits haunt the spirits, not the stone or timber"
Miss Parr stepped forward, revealing her blackened hands from the fires she escaped from, she looked like she had been up a chimney.
The sweet smokey incense drifted across Sam's nose, it took

her straight to the house again, in-fact, everything suddenly shifted around her in a blur. She stood still but the scenery moved around her, shifting quickly like part of a stage show production between scenes.
She was in a dark but familiar room.
Moonlight crept in through the tatty curtains and they blew in the breeze. Floorboards creaking beneath her feet, and something reflecting in the back of the room.

Once again she was faced with the dolls.

Something felt different this time, it was surreal and dream-like. Sam stepped forward slowly.

This isn't real.

A long black streak rose from the darkness in front, it was moving heavily but also completely silent, thin hairs reflecting off the beam of light. Followed by another black shadow, and another.. another.. There was no end until it was met with a bulbous and hideously detailed round shape. The body of a giant arachnid, but it had many heads stemming from where its eyes would be.

Doll's heads, some of them hairless on their heads, some of them weeping, some of them were broken and revealed hollowness, one of them missing an eye.

Another was laughing.

She feeds on your fears, she feeds on your fears, she feeds on your fears.

Sam closed her eyes tight, she sensed light returning around her.
Opening her eyes, she expected to see herself back in the chapel lantern. But she was yet again, somewhere familiar. She couldn't place herself, but she knew it.
There was a haze of tobacco smoke, she remembers the smell. A blurry echo of light radiating from a television set. In front sat an army chair, it was brown and stained, and it smelt like a brewery.
A man slouched there, cigarette in one hand, a beer in the other. Grotesquely overweight and his clothes soiled with stains of all colours from previous TV dinners.
He laughed at the screen that was displaying a blur of colours. He couldn't see Sam, it was like she was peering into an immersive photograph, the lighting and colour of the room reminded her of old family photos that the children cherished in the orphanage.
A small girl walked into the room, she had a long purple t shirt on that stopped at her ankles and was no older than four or five. She was clutching a stuffed elephant. Sam's elephant, it was this revelation that made her realise she was staring at her father.
This memory must have existed in the back of her mind, Miss

Parr had access to her memories like a photo album. But she was able to twist them to her will. What should have most likely been a stained and cheap carpet, was actually a black tar like substance, her feet were sinking into it.

The man (who she refused to accept was her father) had very little hair, his hairline vastly receding, brushing it with his stubby fingers, revealing long fingernails that had thick dirt underneath them.

Sam's child-self was standing in front of the television, blocking his view. He scowled and spat into his ash tray and leant forward.

"You are in my way little girl"

He didn't say this in an angry tone, it was light but very sadistic in nature.

"Mummy put me in the cupboard with the bird man again" the little girl sobbed and hugged the elephant plush to her chest.

"Oh no, my little angel, come here and I'll make it better" he smiled, he grabbed her by the waist and lifted her onto his lap.

The suggestion made Sam's skin crawl, and suddenly the scenery around her shifted again, with a blur and loud overbearing noise.

She was again back in darkness, this was different, it was pitch black, closing her eyes made no difference.

Sam crouched down in a tiny space, her arms were hitting fabric that seemed to be swaying, there were old shoeboxes and toys on the floor. Her instinct, almost like she knew where to place her hands, fell upon a pull chord, a small light filled the space, revealing the inside of a wardrobe..

And then a shuffling noise.
Something invoked further memories and as she turned around she was greeted by a giant figure, it was full of black feathers all over its body as it stretched out in the corner. Its face revealed features that resembled the old plague doctor masks from photos she saw once.
It jumped forward as it made a muffled roaring sound.
Once again, the scenery shifted, she could make out the figure of a woman amongst the shifting memories, perhaps her mother.
Now back in the lantern house amongst the hooded figures, Sam was trembling and could not grasp how it was possible that Miss Parr had complete access to locked doors in her own mind.

      Chaos and confusion swirled around her thoughts, an overwhelming sense of fear as memories had been unlocked. Miss Parr took Sam's hand, and with the other was gripping a knife, it had black fabric tightly wrapped around its handle, crossing and weaving over itself several times. The base of the handle had a small metal ball placed there. The knife was clearly sharp and had similar symbols to the black door Sam encountered in the mansion house.
Sam was too distracted by her own confusion to realise that Miss Parr had begun to cut at Sam's palm, a warm sharp feeling spilled across her hand, blood trickled down and spotted on the wooden floor below.
The people around her were like vultures, sweeping in on her. One by one they would grab her hand and place her palm

against their lips. Each of them felt like they were squeezing from her veins, feeling a tight pull as they sucked from the wound and left blood smeared around their lips. With each visitation, Sam was losing more and more energy.

Sam was pale, she was now on her knees and was trembling with weakness and fatigue. Her legs too weak to stand upon had collapsed under her.

To Miss Parr it seemed like just the beginning, a starter before the main course. As she stepped closed to Sam with the dagger and rested it against her throat.

This is it.

Sam closed her eyes tightly, preparing for whatever death would feel like.

44

THE DAY BEFORE

Victor was focused on the map that lay on the table before him. He was studying every inch of its detail, he rubbed the stubble on his face in thought, the feeling of sandpaper against his fingers did not distract him. He traced a green line on the map, it was a road that would stretch through several towns until it came to a stop at a town on the coast.
There, it has to be there.
The aged man, lay back on the throne-like wooden chair, he took off his reading glasses and rubbed his eyes as he looked at his watch. He'd been awake for nearly twenty four hours, but he was so close to his goal and refused to step down from it.
The room had grown cold, the fire had burned out hours ago and was now smoldering, smoke slowly rising through the chimney.
Victor rose to his feet, there was a slight dizziness as he had stood too quickly after a length of not standing at all. He placed his fingers on the desk to steady himself before moving to the coat hanger in the corner of the dim lit wood panelled room.
This was Victor Albescu's study, most of the space was taken

up by the large oak desk, it was littered with paper and photographs. There were stacks of maps, some of which were old and stamped with library logos, he had to borrow them in his research and hadn't returned them. On the walls were paintings of the old country, his home of Romania, his father had come to England before he was born, in the last six years he had passed and left Victor his entire estate.

It was a fairly large house, six bedrooms, a study, a room where a piano had long been sitting too.

Victor was nearly sixty four, his whole life was devoted to his father's same cause. To hunt those that killed Victor's mother and his-at the time, twelve year old sister.

His father's search had grown cold for at least three years before he died. But he had found out much about the cult that had originated in Romania, the cult had spread like a plague across continents, eventually it found its way to the states, where it grew rapidly and undetected within the political structures.

He was running out of time now, they were powerful and had exceeded in numbers since Victor last confronted a pocket of their group, just outside of Cardiff, Wales.

They were not human, at least of origin, they had cross bred with humans for a long while.

The creatures smuggled themselves aboard large cargo ships originally, way back during the dark ages. They were able to spread the plague of their kind quickly through Europe, the great plague was a great disguise for their growth.

They had been routed out of London, in the history books it

was The Great Fire, but Victor had come to learn about a group of hunters that had driven them out of hiding, they had to burn them out. They scattered once again and some fled to the countryside and remained undetected for centuries.

Victor grabbed his coat, he felt an anticipation in the pit of his stomach, he felt like at last he had tracked a large cluster to this seaside town. He would have to confront them, and destroy the leader of that cluster.
The stories of Vampires and Witches somehow had split apart, the truth was they were one in the same, these creatures had supernatural powers, some stronger than others, depending on how many people they had managed to turn. There was a strict code, a hierarchy. One of the great tricks was their power to summon what they would call Guardians, but Victor had never witnessed this, he had however witnessed the power they had over the human brain, the power to access memories and feed off your own fears.
Victor was terrified of dogs, as a child he was almost killed by one when its owner had let it run loose in the park. His last encounter with one of the creatures still haunts him as they were able to convince Victor that he was being chased by a pack of blood thirsty hounds.
Victor had spent the last several nights reading reports about Ilfracombe, fires had cropped up quite often, people going missing in the area, and mysterious deaths. It had all the hallmarks of an infestation.
He rushed to his gun, the stories about how a vampire is killed

were of course fairytales, they could be killed like any human being, a bullet to the forehead would do the trick, but it would be the challenge of raising the gun before they could counter you.

He counted the bullets left in the revolving chamber, and grasped several bullets from a box that sat nearby, he placed them in the pocket of his shirt.

Stepping outside into the cold and dark night, he was very much aware of his surroundings, the wind howled across the large oak trees that surrounded the property, the large metal gate was whistling as the wind played it like an instrument as it rattled on its hinges.

He stepped towards the gate and unlocked the heavy padlock, pulling at the chain it quickly came loose and he pushed the gates open. Heading up the cobblestone path to his car, he felt the wind was gathering its strength, rain came lashing sideways, Victor could feel the dampness on across his face, but couldn't see it falling, only when looking up at the automatic exterior light on the side of the house as he approached the garage doors.

He pressed a button on his key and this activated the garage door, it lifted with a loud mechanical grind and then a thud. His father's car sat beside his own under a large dust sheet, he was rather fond of classic cars but Victor had no interest. He couldn't bring himself to sell his father's collection and so it was just left untouched in the garage.

Victor had what many people would describe as an old banger. An Citroen BX GTI, black, with a taped on left mirror, it had a

tape deck of course that didn't actually work and the radiator was shot, the starter motor was on its way out for the third time. But Victor wasn't fussed, it got him where he needed to go and he disliked spending money.
He climbed into the car which bounced quite significantly, which also showed signs of the suspension issues it had considering Victor was small and very thin, he observed the smudged rear view mirror, noticing he was looking thinner recently, his high cheek bones pretuding.
After several attempts at starting the engine with the turn of a key, it eventually fired up, the radiator didn't kick in and so he left his coat on and zipped up. He pulled out of the garage and out of the estate, not bothering to close the gate behind him, he had a feeling that this would be his last time at home as he drove on into the dark winding country roads ahead.

It had been an hour since he had left the safety of his home. Victor was very tired and it was most likely dangerous for him to be driving after such little sleep. But his thoughts kept him sharp and aware, he was headed somewhere which could house a large cluster, he would have a fight on his hands, and it could be too late for him to save Ilfracombe from becoming another ghost town.
He had been on a main road for some time, there was very little traffic as the wind continued to smash against the side of the car, at times it proved difficult to keep the car straight and in control, especially as the roads opened up with less cover. Bright lights blurred in the horizon as signs for services on the

left approached, Victor needed a rest and decided to pull in, he wasn't far out from Ilfracombe now and his anticipation, and fear, was growing.

He pulled in, and instantly realised the car park was deserted. Street lights flickered across the tarmac, but nobody was in sight and it made him feel uneasy.

He got out of the car, with some struggle to open the flimsy door in the wind, which also blew his step back as he battled to the automatic doors of the service station. They opened with a wobble, the place wasn't very well lit and there was nobody around, the arcade machines were chiming, music playing softly but not even a lorry driver tucking into a Burger King.

He approached the doorway to W H Smiths, he found his way to the drinks and picked up a bottle of water, strangely there was no staff member at the till either, he used the self checkout and hurried out of the shop.

It had dawned on Victor that he was only thirty minutes out from town, could it be that the cluster had grown this far out? - normally they would restrict themselves to a town for sometime and rather than the circle growing, they'd suddenly pop up two to three hundred miles away in another town.

As he headed over towards the toilets, he caught a scent, it was pungent but he had recognised it instantly. It was a classic calling card of scents that would often accompany something or someone that had been dead for several days.

Victor pushed the toilet door with his knee, instantly greeted with a swarm of flies and a smell that made his gag. A trail of blood hooked from the door all the way across the toilet into a cubicle that was wide open.

He didn't approach it.

"Hello?"

Victor called out, but he knew he would have no reply, he waited seconds and then closed the door.

He didn't run, but he quickly walked back to the car, got in and started it up. He couldn't believe his luck, the car had started on the first try. He wasted no time as he drove away.

45

PRESENT DAY

"Drop the knife"
A confident voice broke through the crowd where Sam sat at her knee's, knife to her throat, the cold steel against her skin was unnerving, unsure if she was even still alive and questioning her entire life at this moment. She was facing away from the voice, Miss Parr looked up towards the source.
"I'll ask again, drop the knife, please"
Victor stood in the doorway of the chapel, the wind and rain howled beyond his shoulder. He was confident in appearance, but inside he was terrified, he had never come face to face with so many of them together, he had never witnessed the rituals he had only read about.
"And who..-"
"My name is Victor Albescu, I've been following you for a long time Florence, you destroyed my family, and now I will return the favour" he interrupted, raised the gun and shot two rounds, each into two of the hooded figures that were drifting towards him.
Sam had a glimpse of hope. Although the ringing of the gunshots had caused an intense ringing in her ears, followed by a moment of vertigo.
Attempting to crawl away, Sam failed this and with clawed

hands she was pulled back by Miss Parr by her feet.
"Let her go"
Victor fired another round into the crowd, as another figure dropped to the ground, a pool of blood emerging from beneath a faceless twitching corpse.
Miss Parr launched a stool across the room towards him, Victor stepped aside quickly, narrowly avoiding the collision. Sam ran for the door, Victor grabbed her by the arm and pulled her behind him, shielding her and raising the gun to Miss Parr.
Then something emerged from the corner of the room, Victor was staring and couldn't shift his gaze, it was his mother. Dressed in all white, a ghostly glow surrounded her. The smell of her rose perfume overcame him, his pull on the trigger loosened immediately.
Sam squeezed his arm, bringing him to the realisation that it was just a cheap parlour trick. He raised the gun back to Miss Parr and fired three shots in quick succession. The chamber sat smoking and empty.
Two of the bullets didn't hit the intended target, one of them was lodged in the wall behind her. Another had smashed a vase perched in the back of the room. The third bullet however, penetrated the palm of her right hand clean through, it bled profusely, but she displayed no pain on her expression, she looked at her wound with curiosity, it was smouldering.
"Your kind are a plague on this earth"
Victor sneered at her, he was taunting now, feeling confident after the wound he inflicted. But his mistake was forgetting

the chamber was empty.

The crowd of hooded creatures swarmed forwards in unison, like a swarm of bats rushing for the night sky. Victor pushed Sam out of the front doorway, he kicked back the figures trying to overcome him, in doing so, the spare bullets in his top pocket scattered over the floor with chiming metallic drones. Fighting his way free, he stepped out and pulled the door closed, holding the handle.

"The lighter, in my pocket!"

he screamed at Sam, who was on the floor, watching the scene unfold in front of her. She scrambled, not to her feet, but forward with her hands, grabbing the lighter out of his pocket and pulling back the lid as it instantly ignited.

Victor opened the door slightly ajar, hands flew out of the gap, desperate to escape or to grab at them, looking like a horde of hungry undead.

Sam tossed the lighter through the gap, and a few seconds later, the hands had retreated.. There was silence for just a moment, like the eye of a storm had now moved overhead.

The lighter flew back out of the doorway, sliding across the floor towards Sam, they both looked at each other, realising their plan had failed.

There was nothing for the flame to catch, they expected it to work like the movies, waiting for a frankenstein moment when the windmill went up in flames and caught the monster inside. The door burst open, Sam and Victor ran down the sloped hill, chased by hooded figures. There was no slowing down, one error would lead to them being caught by the swarm behind them.

They were directionless, running down towards the harbour pier below, the hill seemed taller headed back down somehow. "Keep going.. The car" Victor pointed, but Sam was too focused on not being gained upon. Victor had one bullet left, he was trying to load the chamber while running but it wasn't very successful.

If i could just take out one more, we might stand more of a chance when we reach the car.

His fingers lost grip of the bullet as it dropped out of sight with a distant pinging of metal hitting concrete.

Trying to adjust her speed as they approached the car, it wasn't so successful. Sam slammed into the side of the car, it was painful but she tried to not think about that. Victor followed with a hard slam against the bonnet.

Victor never locked his car, it wasn't a habit but on purpose, but he never knew why. Now he knew, and he was glad of it. They both clambered in, slammed the doors and Victor locked them.

Figures were on the car instantly, slamming against the glass, trying to break it with their hands. The smudged imprints of their palms haunted the glass.

Sam was screaming, it was too intense now and she felt her insanity slipping away, it had held out for a good time.

Victor yanked at the key several times.

Damn starter motor, I knew it would end up killing me, of all things.

"Start it!" Sam was howling, hands still slamming on the

windows all around, Victor realized they had the car completely surrounded and occasionally caught the glimpse of Miss Parr's pale white face peering through. She was just watching from afar, like a full moon observing the lands below.

The car roared to life, he pulled on the handbrake without a moment to lose, hit biting point and slammed down on the accelerator.

The car juddered as the figures outside parted like the red sea, a blurred wave of hooded cloaks swayed out of sight and into the rear view mirror, slowly engulfed in darkness.

They had escaped, all that remained in that moment was a squealing fan belt and a rattling suspension.

Sam turned and looked back at the dark road fading behind them as Victor sighed loudly.

There was silence for at least ten minutes, they drove through a deserted town, reminding them of the pandemic lockdown in which everyone had to stay indoors for weeks on end.

Yet Miss Parr's presence somehow still loomed over them.

"I suspect they'll be hunting us both now"

Victor punched the glove compartment and grabbed his reading glasses, he slipped them onto his face and blinked several times in succession to adjust his eyes to the lenses. Sam stared at his gaunt face, his features were not so different to Miss Parr's sharpness, it came with age she guessed and he had a certain ghostly quality to him as well. But somehow the man she was staring at seemed familiar, she couldn't place it.

"Victor, by the way.. If you hadn't already caught that" he

briefly smiled at her, only taking his eyes off the road for a split second and returned to his blank expression.

Sam watched the cat's eyes on the road speeding underneath the bonnet of the car, the moon was shrouded in clouds, starlight briefly pierced through.

"What…"

Sam struggled with words, she knew what she wanted to say but she felt stupid saying it, even after everything she had been through.

"What are they?"

A brief silence was soon interrupted by his continued explanation.

"Well, people believe all kinds of things. Witches, demons, ghouls, banshee's, lycan throats.."

Sam just stared blankly, she couldn't believe this was a conversation happening between two strangers in the middle of the night.

"Hell, even the cornish folklore talks about fairies and giants up at St Michaels!" Victor laughed to himself.

"But, in my homeland.. There is quite a different legend" he frowned, thinking of the stories his father would tell him as a child. Handed down from his father. And a rhyme.

Hark, hark! the dogs do bark,
Beggars are coming to town.
Some in rags, some in jags,
And some in velvet gowns.

Without realizing it, he was quietly singing it.

Sam's reaction was mute, but her face presented increased fright.

"Yes, quite the flavour of rhyme isn't it - My homeland spoke of another creature, the Nosferatu… Vampire to your culture, you can thank Dracula for that modern slang"

There was a long pause as they drove past the services that Victor had grimly explored earlier that night.

"But, how can these things exist?"

Sam spoke up, her voice was raspy and tired.

"With secrecy, there are a great number of them now, but they hide in plain sight and in positions of high power"

Sam yawned, she was struggling to keep her eyes open and her body was defeated from the scrapes and bruises she had accumulated over the last few days. But she was too frightened to close her eyes now.

"The woman you saw.. who was she?"

Sam pulled herself up in the seat with the remaining energy in her arms.

"My mother, she'd been dead a long while.. Thank god you squeezed my arm, it was a wake up.. Those creatures, especially powerful ones like.. her.. They have abilities that are completely unimaginable, I expect you've seen this yourself?."

Sam nodded, they both frowned and stared off into the road ahead, wondering what came next.

46

The sun was slowly beginning to wake, the blackened sky was slowly becoming a dark blue, the occasional bird flew past the backdrop of fluffy broken clouds.
"They are not afraid of daylight unfortunately, we must continue to be cautious."
Victor slowed as they rolled into the car park of a travellodge, next to it sat a shuttered little chef restaurant, a sign of life in the area many years ago.
They engaged in a conversation about Sam, and where she had come from. She kept her past brief, she was tired of explaining it to people over the years.
"You won't be safe at the orphanage, they've got that place in their grasp now, i fear for the other children"
Victor was concerned, he had not known the extent of their reach within the care system; it allowed them to use it as a blood farm.
"They won't stop now, we should sleep here for a while and move on somewhere else"
Sam was frustrated.
"We can't just run forever, we should face this"
Sam was confident, she had felt as if she had a new found superpower and was feeling positive about herself amongst the

traumatic events that were unfolding in the world around her.
"There is a time for fighting, we can't do this alone. There are others in my network, but we have to be careful not to expose them to the same fate"
Victor tapped the small black book that sat in the driver door of his car, Sam wondered who was listed in there and who would be able to help them.
"I'll get us a room"
They both left the safety of the car, paranoid about their surroundings and Sam felt as if Miss Parr could arrive at any moment.
"You are my daughter, we are visiting your mother who is sick, understand?"
Victor explained, it had dawned on Sam just how smart he was. A man able to think on his feet and make quick decisions.
Walking in through the automatic doors, they were greeted by a tranquil lobby of the hotel. It wasn't fancy, it was in fact very basic, but it aroused less suspicion and Victor didn't carry much money around with him.
"A double room with two single beds please" Victor smiled, a fake persona engulfed his body language and tone of voice. Sam smiled genuinely, she was impressed.
The receptionist was not phased, he didn't look at them with any suspicion, in fact he didn't look at them at all, and said nothing of importance or value, Victor was about to tap his card and remembered that it was traceable. He paid with the only cash he had left in his wallet.

They walked away with the keycard and headed towards the lift.
"Best not to use card, i know it sounds crazy, but you don't know if they have access to track it, they have eyes and ears everywhere Sam"
It felt like a spy movie to her, like she was living in a real James Bond movie.
They circled the first floor a few times, the corridors were identical and Sam felt uneasy as it reminded her of the house. The decor was aged and it had a musty smell that just brought back a feeling of terror.
The room numbers were confusing to them both, they would often stop half way, turn and walk in another direction.
Eventually they found the room, Victor went straight for the handle, smiled and remembered he needed to use the keycard he was given.
"I am little old fashioned, sorry"
They walked into the room, he slid the card into the small slot that powered the room, it took some time after being confused over the light switches not working. Sam thought maybe he wasn't so smart after all.
Sam climbed onto the bed closest to the door, she felt safer that way and it reminded her of being in the closest bunk to the door at the orphanage.
Victor went straight to the window, he was peaking out of the curtains and deep in thought.
"You get some sleep for a bit, and I will keep watch"
It didn't take much persuasion, Sam drifted off quickly to

sleep, and she didn't dream this time.

Sam felt herself waking up, she still had her eyes closed and for a moment she didn't think of anything but the comfort of the bed. A few moments passed, drifting in and out of light sleep, she started to remember.
She shot up in bed, still fully dressed and not even under the covers, she didn't plan to sleep long. The bed next to her was a mound of covers, realizing that Victor was asleep in the bed and snoring away.
A car door shutting alerted her, she stood up and rushed to the window, peeking through the curtains - she couldn't see anybody there, but there were many more cars there now. She looked at the small clock on the mini fridge door. If it was set correctly it was one thirty in the afternoon.
"Victor?"
There was no answer, she decided herself that she wasn't in any danger right now and he could sleep some more. She walked into the bathroom and stood in front of the half wall sized mirror in front of her. She took a moment to observe herself, she stared deep into her own eyes, half expecting her reflection to suddenly do something terrifying.. It didn't happen, she closed her eyes and breathed deeply, for the first time in days she felt safe.
Closing the door softly, making sure to not wake him. Sam quickly took off her t-shirt and observed the cuts, scrapes and bruises on her body. The cut on the palm of her hand was the worst injury sustained. It was a deep red and was throbbing,

she washed it under cold water and groaned at the sharp pain. She glanced at the shower, there was a rush of excitement at the thought of a hot shower and nice shampoo for her hair. It was the first real excitement she had felt for sometime. It made her sad, such a small everyday habit such as bathing shouldn't be such a rarity. But it was.
Emerging from the bathroom, her hair sopping wet, she had to wear the same clothes again, and hoped to ask Victor if they could get clothes from somewhere.
Victor was once again at the window, he didn't turn to look at Sam and continued to turn his eye in the direction of any sound he could hear.
"We should move soon, we've stayed here too long"
He was biting his nails.
"Where will we go now?"
There was a continued silence that stretched on, Victor was thinking of his next move, he seemed focused, like he was deciding on whether to take the prawn with his knight, hoping that he could make a move on the queen next.
"We should move further up into the country, a city perhaps, hide in plain sight like they do, blend in with a crowd"
He continued to bite his nails, staring out of the window through the netting that sat behind the curtains. Hearing a child's laugh past the hotel room door, he panicked. Rushing over to the door and stared through the peep hole.
Sam was worried, but she found his paranoia to be troublesome. But Victor had experience with this, he had seen their capabilities and there were things that Sam hadn't

witnessed yet.

"Time to go"

He wasted no time, he opened the door and Sam rose to her feet, she checked around the room making sure nothing was forgotten, but he was already outside waiting for her.

As they walked towards the lift again, a little girl and her mother walked past and briefly smiled out of politeness.

Victor didn't like it at all and stared back at them. The mother was clearly nervous and hurried her child away in front of her and down the hall.

Is he stupid to think that everyone around him is one of them? Sam felt guilty for thinking it, but she wasn't used to such paranoid tendencies. In studying his movements and impulses, she had come to realise that she was tougher than she gave herself any credit for.

The lift was packed with other people headed up, they skipped over an attempt at squeezing themselves in, and the same happened again for the next.

Victor was tapping his toes, and tapping his fingers against his thigh as he stared at the numbers displaying the floors it was visiting.

Eventually, the doors opened to present an empty lift, they quickly hopped in and headed down to the ground floor, it swung up quickly with a very stern "Exit the lift" automated voice. Sam felt a chill, it sounded like Miss Parr's voice as she left the lift with a lump in her throat.

Victor took the lead, he walked over to a small box and dropped the keycard inside to check out, he made sure to wipe

it first with his sleeve. Sam assumed this was to ensure his fingerprints were not left, and she had internally sighed.
"Breakfast?" a soft phone voice emerged behind them, a woman wearing a shirt with the hotel logo stood with a tablet in front of them. Victor already startled and observed her from afar, he came closer with a hesitation.
"No, thank you, come along" he took Sam by the arm and led her out of the hotel and towards the car, which was now completely surrounded by other cars.
Victor felt like they were being watched now, he observed a statue at the far end of the car park of an angelic figure, he felt the eyes on him, casting judgement and could swear he saw the head move.

47

"Sam?"

Sam quickly turned her head to look at Victor with a puzzled expression. He was focused on the road, eyes not distracted from the coastline they were driving adjacent to.

"Did you say something?"

"No, you were asleep though for a good while"

Victor displayed a smile somehow, the bags under his eyes seemed to be much worse than when they had left the hotel. They had been travelling a good while now, down to the south coast of Devon where red rocks littered the coast. Sam had only just noticed the distinct colouration and was fascinated by it, it seemed like another country to her.

Sam felt a tug at her stomach, and felt a throbbing pain shoot across her forehead, followed by a strong sense of Deja vu. She peered down at her hands, they seemed older somehow, the skin was aged and slightly bruised. *Where did this tag come from?*

A white tag was strapped to her wrist, it had a number digitally printed there under clear plastic.

'46-01 SAMANTHA PARR'

"What.... Is this?"

She peered over at Victor who ignored her, and as she looked out into the road it had morphed into solid white, the car continued to move but she now felt giddy, she imagined this would be how it feels to be drunk.

The car felt like it was still moving, Victor was completely inanimate and focused on what should be the road out of Teignmouth.

Sam pulled down the sun visor revealing the mirror, she looked at herself and saw someone else staring back at her. A bald version of herself, pale with glowing eyes. She screamed in terror, revealing bloody fangs in her mouth, her heartbeat raced up her throat and out of her mouth. Now she couldn't feel her heartbeat, she couldn't see anything but white.

"Sam, just lie back please.."

The white light gradually became smaller, she was in a room she didn't recognise at first. It was off white, reminding her of the paint in the mansion house.

"Sam come on now, we don't want you hurting yourself again" It was the driver, but he was different. Still of the same age, but he was a long white jacket, and wore a grey buttoned up shirt beneath it, there was a name tag "Dr Riley"

Sam began to panic, she realised she was in a hospital gown, but it had a white fabric belt around the waist to keep it well fitted.

The walls were padded.

"You..where have you taken me, where is Victor?" Sam screamed as she clambered backwards on her back, shuffling along aimlessly, she was trying to get away using the strength of her elbows to push her along the cold white floor.

"Sam, there is no Victor, you know this, you've been here before"

Sam clutched at her head, she tried to clutch onto her hair and realised it was short and she would describe it as boy length.

"What have you done to me?"

She scratched at the skin of her neck, she had shorter nails, her hands still old, her feet and legs were older too.

Dr Riley signalled for someone outside the door, another man in identical clothing rushed in. It was Richard.

"You!..you are with her!" Sam screamed and swiped her hand like a claw at Richard, but it would have not even scratched him with those nails. She looked at his name tag "Dr Pierce"

"What is this?"

Dr Riley looked over at the other Doctor with a concerned look. "It's significantly worse today, has she been taking her medication Dr Pierce?"

There was a silence, Dr Pierce equally concerned and frowning. "I am sure of it, we make sure they all take them without fail, we check their mouths to make sure they are swallowing them too"

Dr Riley exhaled, as he did so, there was a group of voices outside the door.

"Oh perfect..just perfect, worst timing possible" Dr Pierce looked out of the doorway and back at Dr Riley.

"I'll go and explain everything to them, god damn board meetings, why do they have to insist on looking into things themselves! They are just bloody pen-pushers!" Dr Pierce let himself ramble on for a moment, he stopped when he noticed

Dr Riley staring back at him with a silent "Are you finished?" expression.

Sam cowered in the corner, she made herself as small as possible.

Both doctors left the room and slammed the door behind them, ensure it was properly sealed, they locked it and examined Sam through the small round window.

A group of suited faces came around the corner with the sound of squeaky smart shoes on marble flooring. To Richard, they were the perfect description of "Pen pushers" some of them were older, middle aged men with swept back hair, designer glasses and suits that probably cost more than his education.

A voice at the front, equally well dressed in a black suit, white frilly button up shirt and a pencil skirt, she stepped out and looked into the room with a hint of pity.

"This one is Samantha, she snapped when she was 15 years old, murdered her foster parents Mr & Mrs Thompson. Butchered a young couple on the side of a road, Simon and Claire. And if you recall the fire of Ilfracombe, that was Samantha, she claimed she had to, how was it said.. Drive out the evil" there was a shocked expression on their faces as she continued to talk.

"Yes, quite the shocking case. Poor girl, she now retells a story of absurd fiction, and she lives in it over and over again, she believes that most people around her are some sort of Vampire creature. And that she is on the run with another chappy" the group collectively chuckled and passed by.

The woman remained, staring through the window at Sam.

Sam raised her head, she felt a presence staring at her, a familiar one. Like an old acquaintance that she never hoped to see again. She looked through the glass and saw the eyes of Miss Parr staring back at her, who smiled and slowly walked out of view.

www.ingramcontent.com/pod-product-compliance
Ingram Content Group UK Ltd.
Pitfield, Milton Keynes, MK11 3LW, UK
UKHW011255300725
7152UKWH00029B/175